POINT CRIME

DEADLY MUSIC

14. MAY 1999

Dennis Hamley

■SCHOLASTIC

For John Westcombe,
ex-colleague and County Music Adviser
extraordinaire, who helped me a lot with this story.

Scholastic Children's Books
7–9 Pratt Street, London NW1 0AE, UK
a division of Scholastic Ltd
London ~ New York ~ Toronto ~ Sydney ~ Auckland

First published by Scholastic Ltd, 1995

Copyright © Dennis Hamley, 1995

ISBN 0 590 13318 7

Typeset by TW Typesetting, Midsomer Norton, Avon

Printed by Cox & Wyman Ltd, Reading, Berks.

10 9 8 7 6 5 4 3 2 1

The Ballad of Little Musgrave and Lady Barnard

As it fell out one holiday
Like many in the year,
Little Musgrave went to church, to pray
And watch the ladies there.

Some of them were dressed in red
And some were dressed in green
And the first of them all was Lady Barnard,
The fairest ever seen.

She cast a look on Little Musgrave
As bright as summer sun
And Little Musgrave knew full well
The lady's love he'd won.

"I have a bower at Bucklesfordbury
Bestrewn with cowslips sweet.
Go there tonight, Little Musgrave,
And you and I shall meet."

But this was heard by the lady's page
And fast away he ran.
"Although I am my lady's page,
Yet I am Lord Barnard's man."

Now swiftly runs the little page,
Unto his lord with speed
Who was feasting then with his dear friends,
Not dreaming of this ill deed.

"If this is true, my little page,
This thing that you tell me,
Then all the land in Bucklesfordbury
I'll freely give to thee.

"But if a lie, my little page,
This thing you tell to me.
From the highest tree in Bucklesfordbury
Then hanged you'll surely be."

Lord Barnard called up his trusty men.
"Come saddle me my steed.
This night I must go to Bucklesfordbury,
For I never had greater need."

He charged his men no noise to make
As they rode along the way.
"No horse shall neigh, no horn shall blow,
Lest our coming it shall betray."

"Methinks I hear the throstle bird,
Methinks I hear the jay.
Methinks I hear my Lord Barnard
And I wish I were away."

"Lie still, lie still, Little Musgrave,
And huggle me from the cold.
'Tis nothing but a shepherd boy,
Driving his sheep to the fold."

Musgrave now turned over in bed,
Sweet slumber his eyes did greet.

But when he woke, who should he see?
Lord Barnard at his feet.

"Get up! Get up! Little Musgrave,
And put your trousers on.
For it will not be said throughout the land
That I killed a naked man.

"I have two swords in one scabbard,
Full dear they cost my purse,
And you shall have the better sword
And I will have the worse."

The first stroke Little Musgrave made,
He hurt Lord Barnard sore.
The first stroke that Lord Barnard made,
Little Musgrave breathed no more.

Then he took out a sharp dagger
That was both keen and smart,
And he has stabbed that fair lady,
A deep wound through the heart.

"A grave, a grave," Lord Barnard cried,
"To put these lovers in.
But lay my lady on the upper hand,
For she comes of the better kin."

Prologue

The two figures crouched behind a bush were keeping watch on the cottage. A light showed dimly in an upstairs window.

The night was warm and gently moonlit; a slight wind ruffled the beech trees edging the small garden. Tranquil though the scene was, nothing could stop the wildly beating heart of the terrified younger watcher: nothing would quell the burning, vengeful anger of the elder.

The elder watcher whispered hoarsely to the younger.

"You cannot begin to imagine what will happen to you if you have lied to me."

The younger watcher's state of mind grew even more agitated. The consequences of that threat could hardly be worse than those of the truth.

The church clock hard by struck one. The light in the upstairs window went out.

"Ten minutes," said the elder.

To the younger, the ten minutes were an eternity. The elder, unnervingly still and calm despite consuming rage, looked fixedly at a gold wrist-watch until one short, jagged word.

"Time."

"Do I have to come with you?"

"You set me off on this quest: you will be here to see its ending. Follow me."

They both put gloves on and crept across the lawn. The elder produced a key from a deep pocket. They stood outside the front door, breathing deeply, preparing themselves.

Six people who thought they were in the know had talked for hours — round and round and getting nowhere. Tension filled the room. The taut, strained faces showed that there was little trust between them and much suspicion.

They were in a small room high up in the Victorian building of the Royal National Conservatoire of Music. Just down the road was the huge construction site which in four years' time was to open as the new Citadel Arts Centre, destined to be the home of the Promenade Philharmonic Orchestra of London and the Royal Classic Theatre Company. In another part of London, the Proms were taking place at the Royal Albert Hall. Throughout the rest of the country, millions of television sets were switched on – not for the Proms, but waiting to see if the Holland of Cruyff and Neeskens could beat the Argentina of Ardiles and Kempes in the 1978 World Cup Final.

Nothing outside their own crisis mattered to these six.

One of them, a man, hardly twenty, compulsively twisted a lock of hair hanging across his forehead.

"How can we live with this? We must come clean about it."

"Who to?" An older man, florid of face, strong and deep of voice, spoke with what sounded like contempt. "I'm the one who's had the greatest loss. I cannot *sleep* for grief; I cannot do my work properly. But I know what people are saying about me. Can you imagine what I feel, let alone what terrors may be ahead for me?"

"Of course you are right." A tall woman in her fifties, with fine features and long hair just turning grey, spoke. To the second speaker, she said, "I think I know what happened that night. I think I know who was there. And I'm appalled. But I don't know for sure. And there are friends involved in this; people I know, love, admire – and, until now, trust. But what can I say? There are God-given talents in this room and I can't be responsible for silencing them." To the younger man she said, "If you were involved, it should cost you dear. Losing a reputation after you've worked hard to get it is bad enough. It's worse if it's gone before you've even started."

"How can I live with myself?" the young man said.

"You'll live with yourself all right," said a small, chunkily-built woman the same age as the young man. Her hair was jet black, her eyes dark brown. "You know which side your bread's buttered. I'm not much impressed by your bleeding heart."

"That's not fair," said the young man.

"My dear boy," said a lean, tall man with sharp

3

features and glittering eyes, "as you grow older, you'll realize that personal feelings and artistic sensitivity aren't the same thing at all." He reached out and put his arm round the shoulder of the chunkily-built girl. "Are they, my love? We all know who *your* loyalty goes to, don't we?"

"Keep him out of this," said the girl, wrenching herself free of his grasp. "He's not here."

The tall man looked round the room, a knowing smile on his face. "Isn't he?" he said.

The young man winced, but still looked steadily at the girl.

"What does he mean?" he said.

"He means, sweetie," the girl replied, "that rats can make sweet music too."

"I'm getting tired of this."

A new voice. The other five turned to the speaker, who sat in the corner. She stood and faced them. She was large, almost matronly. Strength of character swept out of her. She would get her way in most things.

"We're in a quandary of our own making. We know what happened and we all have our suspicions. We know what our right course should be and we also know its consequences to us all. So we are deliberately choosing *against* that right course for fear of those consequences. Quite apart from the obvious results, four brilliant careers would be cut off in their prime; two more may never have a chance."

"But—" began the young man.

"But me no buts," said the forbidding woman. "There's nothing to discuss. As from tonight, our lips are sealed.

This meeting never happened; what really led up to it never happened either. Everything will be explained away and the world will accept the explanation. *No one will ever know*. So nobody here will ever say a word."

The young man bit his lip and was silent.

"We'll agree on this," said the chunky girl.

"We'll shake hands on it," said the tall man.

"We'll swear oaths," said the forbidding woman.

The other five all looked at her.

"Yes," said the fine-featured, greying-haired woman. "We will. That's good."

The forbidding woman stretched out her right arm.

"You're not Brünnhilde now," murmured the young man.

"I will not name what has happened because I do not have to," the woman said. "By not naming it I am already consigning it to oblivion. And I will never refer to it again in any way to any living person, including those in this room. I swear it."

The florid, middle-aged man reached out and grasped her hand.

"And I swear it too," he said.

"So do I," said the chunky girl.

"And me," said the tall man.

"I also," said the fine-featured woman.

Five hands were now joined. Their owners looked at the young man.

"Yes," he said. "You are right. I swear it too. It's gone. Forgotten. It never happened."

His right hand joined the others in a knot they never intended should be broken.

* * *

But something had *happened. The pair, the younger and the elder, had become fugitive, had slipped unseen to a car parked under a tree. Behind them, in the cottage, was first a glow, then fire and smoke, then a fume-filled inferno in which no one could live. Next morning, bodies would be found.*

"*Remember,*" *the elder had hissed.* "*We were not here.*"

1

Katie Summers tightened the bow of her cello, sat and waited. So did the other sixty members of the Hedfordshire County Youth Orchestra. This was the first full rehearsal for the summer concerts and it marked a great moment indeed: world première of a work specially written for them by a composer who really *was* somebody, known all over the world. And he'd done it for *them* and was going to rehearse and conduct it with them as well – on this residential course at Pegham Priory and in the four concerts of the summer tour. On Monday they would be taken in coaches westward to the city of Wardminster to play in the ancient cathedral; on Tuesday they'd make the long journey to the new town of Byron Springs; on Wednesday they would be back in their own county town of Hedford; then to London and the final concert in the Citadel Centre, in the very hall where the great Promenade Philharmonic Orchestra of London usually played. Already Frank had rehearsed the strings and percussion and Liz the brass and woodwind in their separate parts of the new work. Now it was all going to come together.

Katie looked upwards and over her shoulder to where Dave Raggett sat quietly and patiently, his trombone resting on his knees. Dave was from the same school – they went back a long way together. And what now? Were things getting a bit heavy? Oh, she liked Dave a lot. But was it more than that for him? And what would she think if she found it was?

Can't wonder about that now. It's time for Hugo.

And here he came, striding to the dais at the front of the orchestra where a baton and the conducting score awaited him.

And wasn't he *dreamy*?

Nearly a year before, Frank Thurlow, County Music Adviser for Hedfordshire (who resisted all plans by officials to rename him Director of Musical Resources) had talked about his big idea to Liz Woolley, the other adviser. He had worked for three years with Liz and liked her – this quiet woman who lived alone now she was divorced, rushed to her boat on the Blackwater in Essex whenever she had the chance and had a shadowy boyfriend Frank had never seen.

"I've been thinking about the summer tour," he said to her. "I'd like to do some big works. Elgar's *Enigma*, some Brahms, a nice sparky piano concerto – we could get a good young pianist in for that. I want pieces which would really show the orchestra off."

The County Youth Orchestra was the great jewel in Frank Thurlow's crown.

"What about something new?" said Liz. "It must be five years since we commissioned a new work."

"I'm glad you said that, because that's what I'd like above all else. But it's the money. We'll need a whole lot to tempt someone good. I know who I'd *like* to get, though."

"We could get money in large chunks if we put our minds to it," said Liz. "The Regional Arts Board will cough up if we can get the LEA to match it, and Friends of the Orchestra would help. One bank's already paying to hire the hall for the last concert in the Citadel Centre. Try tapping another one. We could afford someone really good."

"Any idea who?" Frank was smiling as though he had the answer already.

"Birtwistle? Taverner? Maxwell Davies?"

"How about Hugo Malvern?"

Liz laughed. "He'd never do it," she said.

"He would for me," said Frank. "We were students together."

"You *know* Hugo Malvern?" cried Liz. Frank was pleased to see her awestruck face.

"Very well once. We were great mates. And we've kept in touch. I'll write to him to see what he says in principle – provided we can get the money."

"Fantastic!" said Liz.

The Regional Arts Board *did* promise money if the County Council would match it and, rather to Frank

Thurlow's surprise, the County did. So did another bank. Friends of the Orchestra – an organization Frank tried to keep at arm's length but to which he often had cause to be grateful – weighed in with a surprising amount raised by a raffle and two car boot sales. Frank found himself with a tidy sum to offer.

Hugo lived deep in Sussex. Frank drove out to see him – round the M25, down the M23 with all the traffic for Gatwick Airport, then striking off deep into wooded countryside and well-kept villages. As he drove, he remembered his old friend and their time together at the Royal National Conservatoire of Music. There were three of them: Hugo, Ken and Frank. Hugo, who came as a pianist but who really wanted to conduct and compose, for whom everybody forecast the really great future. Frank, the solid all-rounder who was never going to make it in the world's concert halls, who early on decided bright lights and jetting between continents was not for him and opted for teaching and an unspectacular though satisfying life. And Ken? Well, what happened to Ken still made him, even now, close his eyes with horror and grief. No one would ever know now what had happened to the twenty-year-old Ken, master of woodwind, on that night in July, 1978.

Hugo, though, had been the Gold Medal student of the year. On both the conducting and composition courses, people were saying there had been no one like him at the Conservatoire this century. He was the new Britten, in the league of Elgar and Vaughan Williams.

When he left the Conservatoire, he settled down to compose, and won a lot of prestigious commissions. Not yet forty, he had written two symphonies and three piano concertos which were performed all over the world and often recorded. His operas *Oisin and Niamh* and *Tam Lin* had been staged at Covent Garden, and in Berlin, Paris, Milan, New York, Tokyo, Moscow and Sydney. Scores of smaller works – string quartets, piano sonatas, works for brass and woodwind – had poured from him. He had crossed the world several times conducting his own music. Film and TV work made him rich. And always he came back to the house near the South Downs to think, recharge his batteries and compose again.

Despite how confident he had been when he first suggested Hugo to Liz, Frank had been quite prepared for a rebuff. Hedfordshire County Youth Orchestra wasn't the BBC or the Royal Opera, and the money available might be peanuts to Hugo. But the letter in answer to the first request still warmed Frank's heart.

> *Frank, I'd be delighted. The sum you suggest is perfectly adequate. For you and the kids, though, I'd have done it for nothing. Come down and see me and we'll discuss it over a jar or two.*

Hugo didn't say in the letter that he had another suggestion to make which would keep until he saw Frank face to face.

Frank sat with Hugo amid shelves of books, the Steinway grand, a synthesizer and piles of manuscript paper. They'd had a long and reminiscent lunch at a nearby pub, then returned to Hugo's house to talk over the project.

"You're doing *Enigma*. What about more variations?" said Hugo.

"Perfect," replied Frank.

"It fits in with something I've been thinking about for a long time," said Hugo. "You've given me the ideal excuse."

"What is it?"

"I want to do a set of variations for full orchestra on an English folk song. I can't get it out of my head. It's *Little Musgrave and the Lady Barnard*. Do you know it?"

Of course Frank did. He'd performed Benjamin Britten's arrangement for male voices with the County Youth Choir three years before.

"It's a marvellous tune and it tells a great story," said Hugo.

He jumped to the Steinway and played an energetic tune with weird, haunting harmonies.

"I *must* do something with it," he said.

"Sounds marvellous," said Frank. He was delighted.

"And what's more, I'll rehearse the piece with your orchestra and conduct it on the tour."

Frank stared at him.

"But your fees are—"

"To you, my fee is waived. Let's say it's included in the commission. And it's for old times' sake."

"Hugo, are you sure?"

"Anything to keep away from Chicago or Bayreuth for a few weeks," said Hugo.

"I'm gobsmacked," said Frank.

He left soon afterwards: he had to reach London in time for a meeting about the National Curriculum. But all the way in his car he was singing folk songs at the top of his voice. He never saw how the smile wiped itself off Hugo's face like a wet cloth wipes chalk off a blackboard as soon as he left. Nor did he see Hugo slump into an armchair and pass his hands over his eyes as if ghosts he never wished to see again had appeared before him.

And now here Hugo was, and Katie couldn't take her eyes off him. Up above, Dave couldn't take his eyes off Katie not taking her eyes off Hugo.

Dave and Katie had auditioned together for the County Youth Orchestra the previous year. They were both doing A-level music at Longways Comprehensive School in Hedford and they had both reached Grade 8 with their instruments. Katie wanted a career in music, but Dave wasn't sure. Like so many musicians, he was a good scientist. Besides, he liked rock and traditional jazz too much to fancy a whole life in the brass section of a symphony orchestra. But he *did* fancy Katie, and sometimes he wondered what a whole life with her would be like. And while he frowned at the way Katie was looking at Hugo, he was detached enough to realize it was replicated by every other girl in the orchestra.

Concentrate. Hugo was talking.

"Well, you look a lot happier than most orchestras I stand in front of," he said.

There was a slight disturbance as players looked at each other in alarm. Was he going to patronize them?

"And with good reason," he went on. "I listened to you doing the Elgar. It was a revelation. Everything came out new and fresh as if *it* was having the world première. To the people I usually conduct it's a boring old hack work they can play in their sleep. And frequently do."

The orchestra, relieved, laughed. But Katie noticed Hugo did not smile with them.

"Make the most of that," he said. "It won't last."

The laughter died. There was an expectant silence.

"To business," said Hugo. "A few words about what I've written for you. Variations on an English folk song, *Little Musgrave and Lady Barnard*. Anyone know it?"

A few hands went up, including Dave's.

"Centuries old," said Hugo. "Collected and written down by Cecil Sharp a hundred years ago. It turned up in America as well – in the southern Appalachians as *Matty Groves and Lady Banner*. It tells a good story. Lady Barnard takes a fancy to Little Musgrave and gets him into her bed. But Lord Barnard's page sees what's going on and tells him. Lord Barnard gets all his men together and they burst in on his errant wife and Little Musgrave. He tells Little Musgrave to get his trousers on because he won't kill a man without any, then he despatches Musgrave, gets rid of his wife the same way and mopes when they're buried together. Racy stuff."

"Charming!" muttered Dave.

"Anyway, it's the tune that concerns us," said Hugo. "It's strong and mournful at the same time, like all the best folk songs. I've set the melody straight for the theme, then there are twelve variations, all quite short. I've put them in four groups of three."

Every face looked at him raptly, taking all this in.

"This is an old traditional song," said Hugo. "And in many ways mine is a traditional work. I've tried to do what composers did before me. You're playing the *Enigma Variations*. What's special about what Elgar did?"

I've got to answer this. I've got to mark myself out from the rest for him, Katie thought.

"The variations are all portraits of people he knew, so he titled each one with the person's initials," she said.

"That's right," said Hugo. "And for one variation in each group of three, I've done the same."

Did he look at me appreciatively then? Katie was suddenly angry with herself. *Oh, stop this!*

"Four variations which are portraits of people. Don't worry – they're no one you know. And you won't find out either."

Greatly daring, a tympanist called out, "Will *they*?"

Hugo laughed. "They may," he said. "And I hope they'll be pleased. All four of them."

He paused and they looked at him, listening attentively.

"I don't think any composer can write without in some way showing homage to composers of the past," he said. "The more I thought of the original tune, this folk melody set deep in the countryside and first sung when life was hard and the elements were very close, the more I thought of places and seasons as well as people. And into my mind came one of the greatest works of all – Vivaldi's *The Four Seasons*. I found myself wanting to evoke Spring, Summer, Autumn and Winter, just as Vivaldi did. And what else did that folk theme make me think of? I remembered marvellous works which capture the spirit of places – *Brigg Fair* by Delius, Arnold Bax's amazing *Tintagel*. Then I knew I was going to write variations depicting seasons, places and people who love them. That was my programme for the whole work. Four groups of three variations."

He paused. There was not a sound in the hall.

"OK, then. After the theme, where I've tried to make sure we bash out the tune so no one will forget it, we've got the first group. One: *Autumn*. Slow, dreamy, lots of plangent, dying falls – deeply nostalgic. Cellos, I want you really singing here. But there's a bit of menace from the brass and tympani as well. Just hints – nasty things may happen come winter."

Yes, I'll make my cello sing, thought Katie.

"Now, the place. *By Cutler's Mere*. Lovely spot."

Katie couldn't prevent a little squeal.

"That's near Hedford," she cried delightedly. "Where I live."

"That's right," said Hugo. "Beautiful, isn't it? Shimmering, delicate strings are needed here. There's a fragile loveliness about this little lake and it's much loved by the subject of the next variation. *To L.M.* Woodwinds, this is your chance."

L.M? Do I know an L.M? Well, if L.M. lives in one of those houses at the edge of the lake, I won't, thought Katie. *Real millionaires' row, that is.*

"On to the next," said Hugo. "*Winter*. Brass, I want some real rasping menace. There are blizzards about and monsters prowling. But there's frost, snow and stillness as well. I want the cold to seep into your bones as you play. After it comes *On Granden Fell*."

The players looked at each other. No, the name meant nothing.

"It's in North Yorkshire," said Hugo. "A bleak, lonely, but majestic place. G.S., of the next variation, is often up there."

They took this information in silently.

"Then we've got *Spring*. Which leads us *In Carteret Woods*, which skirt the North Downs on the Surrey and Kent borders, where you'll often see A.V. of the next variation if you know where to look. And last of all, we're in high *Summer* and I want all the full warmth and richness of this lovely orchestra to come out. So we're ready for *Around London* and then you've really got to bustle and be on your toes for the finale of the whole thing, *To F.T.* Now, F.T. is a deep and remarkable and confident person and this is a deep and – I'd like to think – confident, though I daren't say remarkable, piece of music to fit. And I want you to make it a memory audiences will really take away with them."

Roger Curle, who shared Katie's music stand, whispered to her, "I bet I know who F.T. is."

"Who?" Katie whispered back.

"Frank Thurlow, of course. Him and Hugo, they're mates."

"Frank doesn't live in London," said Katie.

"He's *always* there, nipping off for this and that," hissed Roger. "I bet he wishes he *did* live there."

Well, Frank's confident enough, thought Katie. But is he remarkable?

"So there we are," Hugo was saying. "That's a rundown on the piece I've written specially for you. Let's have a first run-through. Don't worry about making mistakes; I want you to get the whole picture. Remember,

17

this will be the first time *I've* heard it as well."

He took the whole orchestra in with one look.

"I'll give you four for nothing. *Allegro vivace*. And *watch*!"

They did. And the crashing chord which opened *Variations on a Folk Song Theme* (*Little Musgrave and Lady Barnard*) by Hugo Malvern sounded for the very first time in the whole world.

2

Hugo's variations were not the only works being rehearsed on this course. The orchestra spent a large part of the four days playing Brahm's Academic Overture and Dave's favourite, the *Enigma Variations* by Elgar. Kate loved *Nimrod*, that wonderful, moving, swelling melody, but Dave was taken by the last variation itself. "I really feel we matter up here in the brass when we play that," he said.

But as big a highlight as Hugo's arrival on the course came on the last full day. The fourth work was Shostakovich's second piano concerto – sparky and lively enough to suit Frank's taste. In rehearsal, Liz provided the piano part while Frank conducted. But Liz knew she was not concert class. No, Frank and Liz had worked out other plans. And Hugo had been a great help.

Just as they were breaking for lunch, Gwen Fenton arrived. Katie saw a young woman enter the hall as the last chords of the Brahms sounded. Liz had conducted, while Frank listened and then told them what he thought. Frank had his back to her. He saw how all eyes which should have been watching him were looking past his shoulder, so he turned.

"Gwen!" he cried in greeting.

He walked over and brought her forward.

"This is Gwen Fenton, everybody," he announced. "Your soloist in the Shostakovich. Gwen, this is everybody. Meet the Hedfordshire County Youth Orchestra."

A smile lit Gwen's face. Her black hair hung in ringlets.

"Lovely to meet you, folks." Her voice was deep and rich.

Katie whispered to Roger next to her.

"Not another word about us girls and Hugo. Your eyes are out on stalks!"

"Well," replied Roger. "You must admit…"

"A few words about Gwen," Frank said. "Though I don't want to embarrass her. Gwen's just left the Royal National Conservatoire. She swept all before her in the piano course. Isn't that so, Gwen?"

"Let's just say I didn't do too badly," she said.

"And now Gwen's starting a career as a concert pianist. And the bookings are coming, aren't they?"

"Can't complain," said Gwen.

"Gwen came to us," Frank concluded, "on Hugo's recommendation."

At that moment, Hugo himself arrived in the doorway.

"OK, break for lunch," said Frank. "Back here at two

o'clock and this afternoon we concentrate on the Shostakovich."

Katie watched Gwen turn and noticed how she smiled when she saw Hugo. They kissed briefly and then walked together towards the dining hall.

"Tough, Katie," said Roger.

"And for you," said Katie.

"Not really," said Roger. "Totty like that's always spoken for by the rich guys. It's a well-known fact of life."

Katie and Dave sat together under a large cedar tree, between the main house and the accommodation block where the girls slept. The July afternoon was warm and sunny. Several members of the orchestra had paired off and were wandering together all over the grounds. Near them sat the leader, Samantha Belling, her golden hair gleaming, with Roger. The *chunk* of tennis balls on racquets sounded regularly from the courts. Laughter and occasional swearing came from the people on the lawn as they made ineffective efforts to master the frustrating game of croquet.

"Well, what do you think of it all?" said Dave.

Katie gave a sigh of contentment.

"Heaven," she said. "What could possibly spoil this?"

Gwen and Hugo walked past, deep in conversation.

"Cunning devil," said Dave. "He knows what he's doing. No wonder he recommended her."

Katie shrugged her shoulders disappointedly.

"Well, what do you expect?" she said. "Even if he is too old for her."

She watched them as they approached and passed a tree. Gwen still talked earnestly; Hugo said nothing, but stared straight ahead, his face an expressionless mask.

"Funny," said Katie. "That's not the face of a man pleased to see his girlfriend."

She watched their backs as they walked further away. She saw Gwen reach out an arm to Hugo. She saw him push it away with an angry gesture, turn on his heel and walk quickly back to the house. She saw Gwen follow him slowly.

"Well, that didn't last long," said Dave.

As they went back to the house for the afternoon's rehearsal, they saw Hugo's car – inevitably a red Porsche – being driven very fast through the front gates.

Whatever upset Gwen had gone through with Hugo, there was no sign of it as she sat at the piano. She was the alert, absorbed, concentrating professional. Shostakovich came alive; Gwen and the orchestra developed a rapport at once. With Frank conducting and Liz taking notes, they did a complete run-through without a hitch. When it was finished, Frank stepped back, clapping.

"Bravo!" he said. "That was terrific. It will knock 'em cold."

Liz rose and approached with her clipboard.

"Not bad," she said. "But don't get too carried away."

Looking at the weaknesses Liz had noticed took over an hour. At 4.30, Frank finally relented.

"All right," he said. "We'll leave it at that. I want you back here at 7.30. We're going to do a run-through of the entire concert to get the timing right. Here's the running order: the Elgar first, then Gwen comes on and we do the Shostakovich. Then comes the interval. We do the Brahms next and Hugo's piece will be the big finish. OK?"

The murmur round the hall showed they'd not had too much difficulty absorbing that information.

Frank cleared his throat.

"I'm afraid Hugo's been called away urgently," he said. "If he's not back tonight, Liz will conduct Little Musgrave. But don't worry. He won't miss the concerts."

Once again they all broke up. Katie watched Gwen walk away on her own. She also saw Frank and Liz talking as she went. As Katie passed, she was sure she heard Liz say, "I think that girl's brought trouble."

Gwen had indeed brought trouble. It filled Hugo's mind as he negotiated the London traffic, squeezed into the car park at the Royal National Conservatoire of Music, and strode through the doors and up the stairs to the Principal's office.

The run-through went well. They were finished by ten o'clock.

"Get an early night, now, please," said Frank. "We're on the road tomorrow and the first concert for real is in the evening. You've worked hard these four days and I want you all having a good night's sleep."

Pegham Priory was a large old house now used as a residential centre for courses and conferences. All the meetings, teaching, playing, eating and socializing went on in the main house, where there were also bedrooms: some large and rather palatial for lecturers and visitors. Frank, Liz, Hugo and – for the one night she was there – Gwen each had a wood-panelled en-suite room of some size and beauty. So did the members of the Friends of the Orchestra who came on the tour to help Frank and Liz with organizing and taking groups – crabby old Arthur Armitage who used to be head of music in a secondary school; Anita Smith, who was a woodwind teacher; and Ginny Belling, a piano teacher and mother of Samantha, the orchestra leader. Other bedrooms were converted into shared dormitories, with two, four, even six to a room.

The main house couldn't hold all the people who wanted to come to Pegham Priory. Forty metres away were two square, brick-built buildings in which were twenty small single study-bedrooms. It was to one of these that Katie was assigned.

The room was at the front of the building, on the top floor above the entrance, and Katie had a good view of the drive and the front of the house. It was this view that she found herself surveying at one o'clock in the morning.

They had all tried to get an early night. After making hot chocolate in the little landing kitchen, the girls on the top floor hadn't staying talking for long. But Katie's mind was too active to sleep. The sounds of that final magical run-through wound round inside her head. Especially Hugo's variations. She couldn't rid herself of the textures, the harmonies, the rhythms, the sheer physical sensation of playing it. And, though Liz conducted tonight because Hugo hadn't returned, she could not dispel the vision of Hugo standing in front of them, in corduroy jacket and roll-necked sweater, at once casual and elegant, sweeping them all into understanding and sharing the experience his music expressed.

But what *was* that experience? There were so many moods in the work; Katie had been overwhelmed by the switches from fast to slow, loud to soft, major to minor, fat, thumping chords to delicate solos. You were on your nerve-ends throughout this music. Hugo had said the music *described* seasons, places and people. This sounded detached. But was it? What was expressed in it of *Hugo*?

Katie wondered. There were other things in this music which stirred, even frightened her. There was yearning sadness, fear sometimes, once or twice a ripple of menace which disturbed her. She remembered those phrases again – and imagined Hugo's expressive face urging the emotions out of his willing orchestra.

Hugo, Hugo, Hugo! But Hugo was in a different league, a different life, on a different planet. And then there was Gwen. Was something going on between them? Had Hugo recommended her just for her ability on the piano?

Suddenly, Katie's room was lit up as searchlights crossed the window outside. Searchlights? No, car head-lights. She got out of bed, ran to the window and twitched the curtain back. A low-slung sports car stood in front of the main house. As she watched, the head-lights were switched off. She heard the clunk of a closing door.

The car was Hugo's Porsche. Katie saw him in the

light of the lamp over the front door, heard the "beep" of his remote control alarm and central locking, and watched him stride to the house and let himself in with his pass key.

Well, at least he had returned; he wouldn't ruin the tour.

The night was calm, warm. Katie knew she wasn't going to sleep. She stayed at the window, watching the moonlit, shadowy scene.

She saw lights switched on in a window opposite hers. They glowed behind curtains for three minutes, then went off again.

Hugo, thought Katie. He's gone to bed.

Then another light shone through a window a little way to the left – only briefly, as if the occupant had slipped out of bed, switched it on to get bearings, then gone outside.

A few seconds later, the first light went on again. This time it stayed on.

As Katie stood at the window, her gaze travelled across the moonlit grounds, past the oaks and cedars which clothed them, to the kitchen gardens with their greenhouse, the formal rose garden and the croquet lawn. *What a lovely place this is*, she thought. *I'm privileged to be here. And how much further than this will my cello take me?*

She was just going back to bed when she noticed that the light opposite had gone out. The great bulk of the main house stood dark, sleeping, still. *Time for me to go as well*, Katie thought.

She took one last look outside.

And suddenly there was movement. A figure

appeared, running out of the house. In the moonlight, Katie could clearly see it was a girl in a nightdress, dressing gown and jacket pulled over the top. She ran towards the accommodation block from which Katie was watching. But she stopped before reaching it, at the very cedar tree Katie and Dave had sat under that lunchtime. She leaned up against its trunk and subsided until she was half sitting, half lying. Then she put her head in her hands.

Katie could see that not only was the girl crying her heart out but also that she was Gwen Fenton.

3

Katie stayed where she was, looking out of the window. *Go back to bed*, part of her said. *You mustn't intrude on private grief.* Another part said, *You can't just let someone sob away like that and not do something.*

She stood irresolute for a full minute.

You can't go out and talk to Gwen. She's famous – or nearly. And surely she's too old for someone like you, not yet twenty, to help?

But she needs somebody.

It's Hugo who's upset her. That's why you want to go – to have a gloat and wonder if there's a chance for you.

That's rubbish! Just to show it's not true, I'm going.

Katie slipped her dressing gown on and an anorak over it, then shoved her feet into her shoes. Making sure her key was in her pocket, she tiptoed down the stairs and through the brightly lit entrance hall. She eased the glass-panelled door open and made sure the Yale lock was on the latch.

The air in the moonlight was sweet, still and warm. The sound of Gwen's quiet crying reached her from forty metres away. Katie ran across the dewy grass.

"Gwen?" she called softly.

Gwen turned a tear-stained face. Katie half-expected a cry of, "Go away! It's nothing to do with you." Instead, she received a half-smile and, "Hello. You're in the cellos, aren't you?"

"Katie Summers. I'm on the first desk." Katie felt a little surge of pride when she said that – extinguished at once when she reflected how puny that distinction must seem against Gwen's achievements.

"You play beautifully," said Gwen. "I was in a youth orchestra like yours before I went to the Royal National Conservatoire."

"I couldn't help hearing you crying, and I thought—"

"It's all right. I'm better now," said Gwen, wiping her eyes.

Greatly daring, Katie said, "It's Hugo, isn't it?"

Now she really did expect an indignant snort of "What's it got to do with you?" Instead came a sigh. "Is it that obvious?"

"Well, yes," said Katie.

There was an embarrassed silence. *She's clammed up*, thought Katie. But she was wrong.

"I don't know why I bother," Gwen said at last. "With the life he leads and the person he is, it's a case of letting the rabbit loose in the lettuce patch as far as Hugo and women are concerned."

"But he must like you," said Katie. "Frank said he

recommended you for these concerts. So when I first saw you, I thought—"

"That Hugo wanted me here for his own reasons as well? Yes, so did I. But if he did, I've blown it, I'm afraid."

"How?"

"I don't know. I just don't get it. It's something I said. An innocent remark. But he went mad."

"What was it?"

"Last week I was in Leeds, playing Beethoven's Third Piano Concerto with an amateur orchestra. In the bar afterwards, this little fellow with a moustache sidled up to me. I disliked him on sight. He said, 'I'm told you know Hugo Malvern. Will you be seeing him soon?' and I answered, 'Yes, next week,' and he said, 'I've been asked to give you a message for him. He'll know who it's from. Does he remember Ken? He should do, but if he doesn't, not to worry, because Ken will be getting in touch very soon. Hugo's given him the key. Don't forget now,' and then he was gone. I was glad. I didn't want to get stuck with him the whole evening. But I didn't forget the message. I told Hugo as soon as I saw him today."

Katie remembered watching the two of them after lunch.

"Hugo went very quiet when he heard it," said Gwen. "I could see it had made him think. But he'd turned so preoccupied, so cold. I'd built this few days up so much in my mind and here he was just turning me off. And then he said, 'What the hell do you want to tell me stuff like that for?' and just left me. Talk about shooting the messenger! I felt awful."

"It didn't show when you played today," said Katie.

"Of course not. It's my job," said Gwen. "Anyway, this afternoon he got into his Porsche and roared off. Trust Hugo to have a Porsche. He likes people to know he's arrived. There are fast lanes in music as well as in anything else."

"Where did he go?" asked Katie.

"I don't know. Probably London."

Katie laughed mirthlessly. "Another girlfriend?" she said.

"Perhaps," said Gwen ruefully. "Or he might have gone to the Royal National Conservatoire."

"Why?"

"He's always there. He gives one-off lectures, master classes, that sort of thing. That's where I first met him, on a master class. After all, he's their star product this century."

"But didn't you see him when he came back?"

"What makes you think that?"

Kate felt suddenly doubtful. Gwen might be unburdening herself, but she was still the older woman with secrets of her own talking to a humble member of a youth orchestra. Luck shouldn't be pushed too far. But she'd started, so she'd finish.

"Well," she said slowly, "I saw Hugo come back. I saw the lights go on and off – and then you came out. I thought you'd got out of bed, gone to his room, he'd sent you away and so you rushed outside instead of going back to your room."

Gwen laughed. "Well observed," she said. "I couldn't sleep either. I thought he'd gone for good. I couldn't bear it if opening my big mouth had ruined your concerts. But then I heard his car. So I waited until I heard steps in the corridor. I thought he might come straight to my room. But I heard his door open and close; and there was silence. So I got out of bed, went down the corridor and knocked at his door."

She stopped.

"Then what?" said Katie.

"There was no answer. Well, I'd worked myself up to such a pitch I wasn't going back, so I went in. He was sitting on his bed, his face as pale as death. 'What's the matter, Hugo?' I said. He pushed me off. 'Just keep away from me,' he answered. 'I've stirred up something best left alone.' Poor Hugo! He looked *dreadful*. I tried to give him a cuddle but this time he was really violent. '*Get off!*' he hissed. 'I'm on my own in this.' I still wouldn't go. So he stood up and *hustled* me out of the room. There I was, in the corridor, with his door locked against me. I was distraught. What had I done? I *couldn't* go back to my own room; I'd never sleep tonight. I just wanted *out*. So I came out here."

"And I saw you," said Katie.

"You've been great," said Gwen.

"But I've not done anything," said Katie.

"You've listened. Just *saying* this makes me feel better. I think I can go back now."

Katie felt disappointed. She had hoped they might talk for a while.

"But what's it all about?" she said.

"I've no idea," Gwen answered. "Hugo's a public figure but he lives a very intense private life. He knows everyone in the musical world and a lot outside it as well. There must be hundreds he's upset over the years – and who've upset him as well."

That sounded like the end. Katie tried to think how to keep the conversation going. But Gwen spoke again.

"Look, this is between you and me, right? I don't want *anyone* to know. OK?"

Suddenly Gwen was the older woman talking to the young girl. Not for the first time, Katie felt the gap between them.

"OK," she said.

"I'm getting cold," said Gwen. "I'm going back. I think I could sleep now."

They said good night and returned to their respective rooms. Katie had a lot to think about as she climbed into bed, but she slept in the end and woke remarkably refreshed, ready for the new day and the first concert.

Katie watched Hugo carefully as he came down to breakfast. She saw him go up to Frank and Liz, talk to them, laugh. He nodded genially to the Friends of the Orchestra sitting with them. Samantha's mum gave Hugo a shy smile, Arthur Armitage looked away – Katie thought disapprovingly – while Anita Smith seemed ready to walk away with him there and then. Hugo looked perfect as usual, moving easily and confidently.

Gwen dashed into breakfast late. She looked a wreck. She never spoke to Katie, and avoided looking at Hugo as well.

After breakfast, they cleared their rooms and packed. By eleven, they were all in front of Pegham Priory as their instruments were carefully loaded into the luggage holds of the two coaches which would take them to Wardminster and the first concert.

Katie sat next to Dave. Gwen sat with Liz at the front of the coach. Frank was on his own. Where was Hugo? The answer came as the Porsche roared off in front of the coach.

Frank stood up.

"Don't worry, folks," he said. "Hugo will be with us to set up in Wardminster cathedral."

The journey down the M3 to Wardminster took two hours. Before they left the coaches, they ate the packed lunches provided by the kitchen staff at Pegham Priory. After they had left their things in the Youth Hostel and claimed their bunk beds in the dormitories, they started the long afternoon job of setting themselves up in the cathedral, in the wide space at the top of the nave. At last the raised blocks, chairs and music stands were in place in front of the superb wooden mediaeval rood screen.

Now everything was to Frank's satisfaction. He looked at his orchestra.

"Right," he said. "Now it's for real. A real concert, a real audience and a real world première. Don't worry: you'll be great. And Hugo *will* be here."

Did Katie detect a slight desperation in Frank's voice there?

They only rehearsed starts that afternoon. Katie noticed how different sounds were in the huge echoing place compared with the small rehearsal room in Pegham Priory.

Eventually, Frank was satisfied.

"Well done," he said. "Have a look round the city till five. Early supper at the hostel, then it's here and ready for action at seven sharp. God help anyone who's late."

Katie and Dave wandered together round the mediaeval streets in the old part of the city. She wondered how far she could let him in on last night's happenings. No, she decided. I promised Gwen. But I'd *love* to know what Dave would think of it.

Supper came and went. After it, Katie had a terrible thought.

I've not rung home for five days.

She rushed to the payphone. There were already six people in the queue: there were some other guilty consciences. No sooner did she start to wonder if it was worth it than ten more were lined up behind her. So she daren't lose her place.

At last her turn came.

"Hello?" Her brother Ricky.

"It's me. Look, I've no time now; there's a huge queue behind me and they're all muttering. Tell Mum everything's great and I'll try to ring first thing tomorrow morning before we leave."

"She's a bit narked because you never rang."

"Tell her I'm sorry. I'll talk tomorrow. I must go now."

She put the phone down. She'd have to ring before eight-thirty tomorrow to make sure they were at home. *Why* had she forgotten? No time to feel bad about it. She had to change into her long dress and be ready.

Seven o'clock. Before they met in the vestry to form up

35

and troop out through the chancel and the rood screen to their places, they watched early arrivals making the most of the clear, limpid evening in the cathedral close. Katie stood with Samantha.

"Who's that my mother's talking to?" said Samantha.

Katie followed Samantha's gaze. The tall blonde woman who was Samantha's mother was talking earnestly to an elderly man, heavily built though certainly not fat, with silver hair and dressed immaculately in a cream lightweight suit.

"Very distinguished," said Katie.

But what happened next was less distinguished than surprising. Hugo suddenly appeared in the crowd.

"Thank heavens he's turned up," said Katie.

Still in casual clothes, he walked purposefully across the close straight to Sam's mother and the stranger. With only the merest nod to Mrs Belling, he pulled the stranger away and walked off with him, talking quietly but obviously urgently. The stranger said nothing until Hugo had finished, then appeared to say no more than three words. He turned, went back to Sam's mother and continued talking. Hugo followed and spoke what were obviously words of apology. Mrs Belling smiled and touched his arm in an "It doesn't matter" gesture. Suddenly, a smile spread across Hugo's face and he shook Mrs Belling's hand vigorously. Then he walked back, past Katie and Samantha and all the other orchestra members who had ventured outside, his face shorn of its smile and now set and serious.

"That was really rude, what he did to my mum," said Sam. "I'm going off Mr Malvern."

"I think something's worrying him," Katie replied.

It was time to go back into the vestry for a final pep talk from Frank and Liz. The close emptied; the audience was in place. Everybody lined up, then, at a word from Frank, they filed out through the chancel. They entered to applause and felt the tension and expectancy in the air.

An oboe sounded a single note and for the next few minutes the air was filled with the sound of tuning up. When all was ready renewed applause rolled round the cathedral as Samantha took her place to the conductor's left.

There was silence. Then Frank entered, in his black tails and white tie, resplendently different from his usual comfortable and slightly rumpled figure. He strode to the rostrum, bowed to the audience and raised his baton. In the absorbed quiet which filled the cathedral came the first notes of the *Enigma Variations*.

4

The interval was here. So far the concert had gone well. The *Enigma Variations* received a performance which pleased Frank as much as it impressed the audience. In the Shostakovich, Gwen had been terrific, Katie thought. She had watched in vain for signs that Sunday's experiences had told on her – there were none. Nothing had stopped this woman with long, shining black hair, in her evening dress of such a rich royal blue, in her progress to the appointed end of a great work.

So here they were, back in the vestry where usually bishops, priests and choirs robed themselves. They drank coffee from plastic cups and talked excitedly. Gwen was flushed with delight at her reception; not even her generous repetition of "A soloist is only as good as her orchestra" could reduce it.

But Hugo, Katie noticed, did not congratulate Gwen. *She wants him to*, thought Katie, *but he won't*. Instead, he was talking to Mrs Belling – and, to Katie's surprise, like an old friend, not a so far barely-noticed stranger.

Time to go back.

They filed in, tuned up, and waited for Samantha and then Liz, who conducted the Brahms. Once again the applause, then the quiet, then the start of the piece.

Katie always loved playing the Brahms. The orchestra really seemed to get it together here; that supposedly gloomy old German knew what he was about, she reflected as the last chords died away and the applause started.

But even as Liz left the platform and the wait for Hugo started, Katie forgot the Brahms. For now the biggest moment, the première of *Variations on a Folk Song Theme* (*Little Musgrave and Lady Barnard*), was here. The work had come to mean a lot to Katie as well as to everyone else, and now, as she sat next to Roger, her cello resting comfortably against her, she thought again about the piece she was about to play.

Those places. Those people. How odd that the first place to be written about was so near her home. Did the ducks and coots and moorhens on the surface, the bream and tench and pike in the depths, have any notion what their home had suggested? And what about L.M., who, Hugo said, loved the place? Was L.M. there now, striding round the little lake's shores? Had L.M. any idea of what was happening here in the cathedral at this very moment? Could L.M., by any chance, be in the audience? Somehow, Katie doubted that.

The moment was near. Almost instinctively she looked

upwards, towards the brass and Dave with his trombone. Their eyes met: a little smile of encouragement each to each. Then, eyes front again, and the roll of applause as Hugo Malvern, also in white tie and tails, came to the rostrum.

Hugo raised his hands. The audience was still. Every eye in the orchestra watched him. Every hand, every tensed bow, every caught breath was ready. With a great swooping movement of hand and baton, he brought the orchestra in to the first fortissimo crashing chord. Then Katie found herself lost in the swaying, easy rhythm she was maintaining with the other cellos and the double basses as the woodwinds and violins pattered out the simple melody.

Yes, they were now launched on a journey. The car had left the garage, the train had drawn out of the station, the harbour breakwaters were slipping away behind the ship. Hugo was leading them on an adventure and no one had trod this way before.

Laura Merchant looked at her watch. The day had been hot, but the evening was cool and a pleasant breeze rippled the waters of the lake in front of her house.

Where was George? She always worried when he took the car into town. "I'll be back by six," he always said – but he never was. There were too many pubs selling too much good draught bitter. And George was no drunkard but he liked his talk and he liked his pint and he was no good with time. One day he would climb into his prized old classic Riley saloon feeling on top of the world, and a policeman would be there to ask him to blow into one of those things – and that would be that. Could a man of 76 get his licence back? And what would they both do without George to drive the car?

Elder brothers could be a pain. For three-quarters of a century, for Laura it had been so. And yet: now husbandless and wifeless, having been their separate ways all round the world, here they were together, living out time in the house by the lake.

It's summer outside, *thought Laura,* but it's autumn in my mind. *Voices from years back seemed to sound inside her head.* "It's always autumn with you, Laura."

"Oh, come on, George. I'm getting worried."

First variation. Autumn. A gentle but slightly threatening phrase started in the cellos and double basses and was taken up by the brass. Katie stole another glance over her right shoulder as the trombones repeated the figure. Dave was there, his eyes fixed seriously on the open score in front of him. All through rehearsals she had the fancy that at this point she was sending a message on her cello and he was answering it on the trombone.

Now came the main theme: pizzicato on the violins, like a sudden shower. Then minor chords presaging gloom and the end of things, though the piece was only just beginning.

The three Siamese cats, Miaoshan, Tian Hou and Confucius, waited for their supper – two dainty lilac-point females and a lean, mean-looking seal-point male. Their blue eyes watched Laura intently as she opened a tin of Whiskas and spooned equal shares into their bowls.

"You have yours," said Laura. *"But I have to wait for your naughty uncle to come back before I can have mine."*

Second variation. *By Cutler's Mere.* The tremulous sound of stopped strings making a foundation as the solo oboe wove little arabesques and curlicues on the original theme made Katie recall clearly the lovely little lake round which, that summer, she and Dave had often walked. Trees down to the edge, swans in the water, coots in the reeds, houses on the far shore with lawns stretching down to the water, little jetties with boats tied up to them.

"Whoever lives here?" she often said to Dave. "It's so beautiful."

"Out of our league, love," Dave would reply.

"One day," Katie would answer. "One day. You'll see."

Well, Laura lived there now. The three beautiful cats were eating. Laura walked into the drawing room. The Bechstein grand gleamed darkly, Beethoven sonatas open and ready to be played. Framed photographs of faces dear to Laura covered the walls. Strangers would have found many familiar.

They brought back such memories, not all happy. Only that day the recollection of one had shaken her. A phone call – from Hugo Malvern after so many years. His picture was on the wall – face young, unlined. She had followed his career with joy: she knew he would go far. But this was no call of nostalgia. Hugo seemed almost incoherent. Was he drunk? He babbled on about that awful time, those terrible events, so long ago now.

"Why?" she had said. "It's all laid to rest. Let sleeping dogs lie."

He had rung off, leaving her feeling oddly disturbed.

The phone had rung again half an hour ago. She answered, expecting either Hugo again or George to say he was on his way. But there was silence after she spoke and then the receiver at the other end was replaced. That was very unsettling.

Laura stood at the open french window and looked across the lawn to the lake. Dusk was falling. The cats had finished. Confucius rubbed his wise, sharp face against her leg. Miaoshan and Tian Hou cried soulfully for more food.

A car passed outside. It slowed; she heard the gear-change downwards. She bent to Confucius and scratched the top of his head.

"Uncle George is back at last," she said.

But Confucius did not seem pleased. The fur on his spine stood up and his tail swelled like a furry poplar tree.

Katie loved the third variation. The theme was split into terse, three-note phrases which scurried restlessly up and down, swapped between strings, woodwind, brass, curiously at odds with the calm waltz rhythm the cellos, basses and percussion were giving. Katie found the effect fascinating. Sometimes, when the three-note phrase was repeated high up by violins or flutes, she thought she heard cats crying.

To L.M. If this was a portrait in music it was of an interesting person indeed. The weirdly busy theme soaring over calm repeated figures – what did that show? A person serene, yet striving and achieving at the same time? Were these separate qualities peaceably united? Were they at odds? Did this person have an internal struggle?

Katie was sure that if the person did, the struggle was not resolved. The variation seemed to stop suddenly, almost in mid-phrase. There was a sudden, almost shocking, silence before the bleak bassoon and trombone chords of *Winter* started.

George eased the old Riley into the garage, switched off motor and headlights and sighed angrily to himself. He'd not meant to fall victim to the hoppy charms of Griswold's Old County Bitter in The King's Head, not meant to have to drive home with exaggerated care in the dark. Now Laura would be angry and make him feel like a naughty little boy again.

He was still shaking. That white BMW had nearly scared him out of his wits, shooting suddenly out of the lake road as he was turning off the main road. Twerpish driving by an idiot. Still, such things were common now. Perhaps it was time to give up.

He locked the car and the garage and walked to the house. Silence except for breeze and lapping water. Laura wasn't playing the piano: no bell-like notes fell though the open french windows.

No cats either. One or other usually met him.

"Laura!" he called.

Confucius leapt at him from nowhere, bit his hand so it drew blood and ran off yowling, tail fluffed out.

"Confucius," George said, mystified. "You never do that."

He wrapped a tissue round the reddened tooth puncture mark.

"Laura?" he called, questioning this time.

He searched every room in the house. It was empty of humans.

Puzzled, George stared across the lawn. A pale, tiny ghost moved in the grass by the water. There was a switch for floodlights over the lake frontage: he put it on. The tiny ghost was Miaoshan, running low and frightened across the lawn.

"Laura!" Now his voice was sharp. What silly game was this?

He strode across the lawn and stood on the little jetty. He looked far over the waters of Cutler's Mere, away from the lit houses, to the place where woods came to the water's edge and night creatures began to stalk.

Then he looked below, to where lake water plopped gently against the jetty. And only now did he see Laura. She lay floating, dead, a bullet-hole in her forehead, white hair fanning round her, long dress sodden, saved from sinking in this shallow water by the tape tying her wrist to a wooden pile supporting the jetty.

Winter was here. Katie found little joy in this variation, no let-up in its harshness, no hint that spring would ever dispel its mood.

5

The first concert was over; the delighted applause still rang in everyone's ears. Gwen and Hugo were not with them; after congratulations and good nights, Hugo had departed to a hotel and Gwen had followed him. Homely though the Youth Hostel was, nobody was surprised at their defection.

Katie and Dave were talking to Samantha, who had an odd tale to tell.

"You know that man talking to Mum before the concert? Guess who it was."

Katie and Dave confessed to not having a clue.

"Sir Gerald Swordblade," said Samantha triumphantly. "He's the Principal of the Royal National Conservatoire."

"How does your mum know him?" said Dave.

"She was a student there once," Samantha replied. "She could have gone a long way if she hadn't had me and then got married. But the weird thing is that she knew Hugo there."

"Why didn't she tell you?" said Katie.

"I suppose she didn't want me wittering on about it, especially if he didn't want to know her. After all, he was the great success and she was the drop-out. He certainly never knew her till he saw her with this Swordblade man. And she'd never have talked to Sir Gerald unless he'd recognized her. That's not bad, remembering her after all these years."

"Was your dad a student there as well?" asked Kate.

"No way," Samantha replied. "And he wasn't my real dad either. He was a lot older than mum. He married her after she had me."

"I see," said Katie, rather at a loss for words.

"He was great," said Samantha. "Only he died last year of cancer. We're on our own now, Mum and me."

She seemed remarkably matter-of-fact about this, Katie thought.

"That's why she wanted to come on this tour," Samantha continued.

The conversation was interrupted by Roger, Katie's fellow first-desk cellist, looking for Samantha. But then, thought Katie, Roger's always looking for Samantha.

"It's strange," Katie said to Dave. "I keep on picking up little snippets about Hugo. Ever since he left Gwen and roared off in his car. He's a very worried man, I'm sure of it."

"Why?" said Dave.

Gwen's not here, I can trust Dave; so I'll betray a confidence, Katie decided. So she told Dave everything.

He listened intently. Katie knew he was sorting out questions which would help her put things into a pattern.

"Is that it?" he said when she had finished.

"Apart from Hugo and Sam's mum this evening," said Katie.

"So all it is is that Gwen turned up here thinking not only would she play for us and earn a few bob but she'd also have a day or three with Hugo. Then he goes off her very quickly when she gives him her message. Some weirdo up in Leeds tells her an old mate of Hugo's wants to get in touch. Doesn't sound like a reason for worry to me."

"It depends on who this person from the past is. And Gwen did say, 'Now he's given him the key.' What does that mean?"

"It could mean anything."

"But why did Hugo dash off?"

"To keep out of her way, of course," said Dave.

"But Gwen said he might have gone to the Royal National Conservatoire. If he did, it's a big coincidence that the Principal of that very place turns up last night and Hugo hurries him off, being rude to Sam's mum in the process."

"There's nothing strange about that," said Dave. "He runs a music college. He probably often goes talent-spotting to gigs like this. Perhaps your name's in his notebook already."

"Dave, why can't you be serious?" Katie said.

Dave answered irritably.

"Because it makes me puke," he said. "You're all obsessed with this man. He's not some romantic hero with a hidden cross to bear. He's just a big creep. Everything else is in your imagination."

Katie didn't answer him. She looked at her watch.

"Time for bed," she said.

At eight-thirty the next morning, Katie was phoning home as promised.

Ricky answered. Before she could say a word about the concert and how she was, he burst out with news of his own.

"There's been a *murder* in Hedford!" he babbled. "The milkman told us. Then we heard it on local radio. There's going to be house-to-house enquiries by the police and *everything*."

"Who's dead?" asked Katie.

"Some old lady. She was shot through the head and her brother found her floating in the water tied up to the jetty."

Suddenly, Katie was interested.

"Water? Jetty? Where was this?"

"On that little lake. You know – Cutler's Mere."

There was a strange feeling in Katie's stomach.

"Who was she? The person who was murdered. Who was she?"

"She used to be a famous musician, the milkman said. She lived with her brother in a posh house by the lake. That's where she was found."

"What was her name?"

"Oh, they did say. What was it? Merson? Merton? No, Merchant. That was it. Laura Merchant. Katie? Katie, are you still there?"

But Katie had put the phone down. Her head was spinning. One thing and one thing only hammered through her mind. Variation 2 – *By Cutler's Mere*. Variation 3 – *To L.M.*

"It's got to be coincidence," said Dave.

Katie was not yet prepared to believe that.

"I wish Gwen would turn up," she said. "I'd love to ask her what she thinks."

"Be careful," said Dave. "You've got something on her. In the cold light of day she won't like that."

The same thing had occurred to Katie.

"Anyway," said Dave, "you won't see her till tonight. She bunked off with Hugo last night and if she plays her cards right the next we'll know of her is when he roars up in his Porsche."

"You're right, I suppose," said Katie. "But there is someone else I could talk to. Sam's mum."

Katie managed to see her as they loaded instruments and cases on the coaches. Dave was with her – "To make sure you don't make an idiot of yourself," he told her.

"Yes, I heard about the murder on local radio," said Mrs Belling. "What a coincidence that it was at Cutler's Mere."

"Did you know Laura Merchant?"

"Oh, yes. She taught piano at the Conservatoire when I was there. She was a concert pianist in her own right as well. Not in the real top class, but she did lots of recitals, radio work, recording, that sort of thing. I'm really upset about this. Who'd want to murder a gentle soul like her?

I wish I'd known she lived in the county."

"But don't you see?" said Katie. "*By Cutler's Mere. To L.M.*"

"Oh, dear," said Mrs Belling. "That's a *very* nasty thought."

Dave spoke.

"Did that Sir bloke you talked to last night say why he came?"

Mrs Belling laughed.

"Gerry Swordblade? He was just Dr Swordblade when I knew him. And he wasn't Principal then, either. He was Professor of Composition. He taught Hugo everything he knows."

"But why was he here?" persisted Dave.

"No reason. He'd just heard about the concert so thought he'd come informally, as a member of the audience. He wanted to hear Hugo's new work and pay his respects to Frank."

"But did he talk to Frank? I didn't see them together," said Katie.

"You're right, he didn't," said Mrs Belling. "Frank didn't even know he'd been there until I told him."

Samantha appeared.

"Come on, Mum," she said. "You're supposed to be helping, not encouraging these two layabouts."

Dave was wrong about Gwen. She was not destined for the passenger seat of Hugo's Porsche. At the last moment, she ran breathlessly through the gates of the Youth Hostel, carrying a hold-all. She was just in time: Frank and Liz had done the final head-counts.

"Gwen!" said Frank delightedly. "Lovely to see you. I thought you were going with Hugo."

Gwen shook her head and subsided into a seat at the front to get her breath back. Katie studied her face to detect her mood, but Gwen's lips were clamped tight together and she made no movement for the whole of the journey.

Kate wondered: *Has she heard? What does she think?*

They were bound for Byron Springs, a new town eighty miles to the north. Once out of Wardminster, the coach headed up the motorway. Two hours later they were passing the industrial estates and retail parks of Byron Springs, then through grid-pattern roads lined with new houses. Finally, they arrived in the wide thoroughfares amid the glass towers of the town itself.

The concert was to take place in the Leisure Centre and this time the orchestra was to stay in a modern conference centre adjoining it. No bunk beds in dormitories, no simple though adequate hostel food – Hugo would have no need that night to go to a hotel. Katie was determined to have a word with Gwen, and as soon as she had dumped her bag and cello case in her room she rushed into the foyer to look for her.

Gwen was looking vaguely at a notice-board. Katie could see she was taking nothing in. Should she break into this reverie? She must.

"Excuse me, Gwen," she said tentatively.

Gwen turned.

"Oh, hello," she said.

Straight to the point.

"Did you hear what happened last night on Cutler's Mere?"

"Yes," Gwen replied. "Poor Laura. I can't believe it."

"What does Hugo think?"

Her mouth was tight shut again. But, after a moment, she spoke – almost, it seemed, with difficulty.

"I don't know what Hugo thinks."

"But have you noticed? Cutler's Mere. L.M. The person in the music murdered in the place of the music, just when the music's being played for the first time in public."

"I'm not daft," said Gwen. "I don't need you to tell me."

"Sorry," said Katie and moved away.

But Gwen moved too, very quickly.

"No, Katie, *I'm* sorry. I mustn't snap at you. I don't know what Hugo thinks because I don't know where he is. He never spoke to me last night and he drove off this morning after breakfast when he heard the news and I don't know if he'll be back for the concert."

"Did you know this Swordblade man was going to turn up last night?" said Katie. "He was Principal of your college, wasn't he?"

"Yes, dear old Gerry." Gwen's face softened into a smile. "I had no idea he'd be there. What a lovely surprise. He's a great man. And he doesn't forget his students. Whether they end up conducting at the Festival Hall or teaching piano to snotty-nosed kids in Middlesborough, he remembers them all."

"He remembered Samantha's mum," said Katie.

"Was she at the Royal National?" said Gwen in

surprise. "What does she do now?"

"Teaches piano to snotty-nosed kids in Hedfordshire," said Katie.

"Well, there you are, then," said Gwen. "It was lovely to see him last night. He must be just about ready to retire. He's well into his sixties."

"Did he say why he'd come?" said Katie. The reason given by Samantha's mum didn't sound enough to her.

"Term's over. He's going up north to a holiday cottage he's got in Yorkshire. He thought he'd delay going till today when he heard there'd be so many old students all together in one place last night in Wardminster. He's on his own now – has been for years. His wife was killed years ago. A terrible accident."

"Hugo didn't look too pleased to see him," said Katie.

"I think I'll give up worrying about Hugo," said Gwen.

Katie didn't believe that. She changed the subject.

"But what about Laura Merchant being murdered? Do you think the police will come here?"

"Why should they?"

"*You* know. Because she was killed just as we were playing that particular music."

"But that's just a very unfortunate coincidence. She probably surprised a burglar who turned nasty. That doesn't mean the police want to see people who were miles away at the time."

Katie had no answer to this.

"If it's a coincidence, then there's no point," said Gwen. "And if it's not..."

"Yes?" said Katie. "If it's not?"

"Well, I don't know. What do you expect? Someone with the initials G.S. to be killed tonight on Granden Fell?"

"That would prove it," said Katie.

Put like that it seemed impossible. But Gwen suddenly went pale.

"Oh, my God," she said. "G.S. Gerald Swordblade. And he's off to his holiday home in Yorkshire. He'll be there by now."

"What do we do?" said Katie. "Go to the police?"

"We'd look silly. They'd laugh."

"We've got to do *something*. Even if we do look silly."

Gwen was thinking.

"You're right," she said. "Come with me."

Katie followed her upstairs to her room. Gwen let them both in, then started rooting about in her case.

"My Filofax," she said, producing the bulky document. "Can't live without it." She flicked through the pages. "Do I have his Yorkshire number?" she said. She cast her eyes down the page.

"Yes!" she said triumphantly. "Got it. Come on. We'll ring him before I settle down to my daily practice."

Katie realized that, whatever the crisis, even for someone as talented as Gwen, the regular chore of hours at the piano never ceased.

They rushed downstairs, to a payphone in the foyer.

"Will he be there yet?" said Katie. "It's a long way."

But Gwen had already put her money in and dialled. She waited, listened, then turned to Katie.

"It's a machine," she said.

She waited again, then spoke.

"Gerry, this is Gwen. What I'm going to say sounds daft. Don't be cross with me if it's a lot of rubbish but I've got to tell you. You know poor Laura was murdered last night? Well, it happened at exactly the same time as you were listening to Hugo's new work. *By Cutler's Mere* and *To L.M.* It's just a thought – but tonight we're playing it again and you know what comes next, don't you? *On Granden Fell* and *To G.S.* Well, you could be G.S. and you're going to be near Granden Fell. I know it sounds ludicrous, but if there's a nutter about, please watch yourself and be careful. Take care, Gerry. It was lovely to see you last night and a real surprise."

She put the phone down.

"We can't do any more," she said.

6

The Leisure Centre hall was huge, like an aircraft hangar. Stewards were still pulling chairs in rows, covering the markings of the basketball courts. The acoustics were different again from Wardminster Cathedral. Frank wanted a full run-through this time. Some players groaned, but he was adamant.

"You did well last night," he said. "But I don't want you complacent so that the second night gets sloppy. Get your sloppiness out of your systems this afternoon."

So the whole programme was played through. Both Frank and Liz seemed tetchy, hypercritical. Katie wondered if much of this was due to Hugo not being there.

At last they were through and Frank let them go to wander round the shopping malls until the evening meal in the conference centre. Katie told Dave about her conversation with Gwen that morning and Gwen's message.

"Yes, it's probably silly," said Dave. "But I suppose you can't be too careful."

Hugo arrived just before dinner.

"Sorry again," Katie heard him say to Frank. "Pressing business. But you know I'll never let you down for the concerts themselves."

After the meal, Gwen spoke to Katie again.

"I tried to ring Gerry again just now," she said. "But it's still the answering machine."

"You did your best," said Katie and went upstairs to change for the concert.

Gerald Swordblade had driven back to London after the previous night's concert. There was much on his mind. It had been a big but welcome surprise to see Ginny Belling again — Ginny Brown as was. He remembered her well: a pianist of great promise until she got herself pregnant, met that fellow Arthur Belling, and retired to obscurity in the country, taking in the children of hopeful parents as unwilling pupils. Still, her daughter Samantha was obviously a capable violinist. One for the future there? And the way she sat as she played and looked so intently at the music in front of her — little bells rang in his mind. Why? he wondered.

Frank Thurlow looked in his element. Thank God for rocks and beacons in a shifting, changing world. And doing such good work. What a pity they hadn't had time for a real talk.

But Hugo? Oh, Hugo! Whatever are we going to do with you?

Gerald Swordblade left his maroon Jaguar in the car park

*of the Royal National Conservatoire, and ascended in the lift
to his flat on the top floor. He had lived alone since the death
of his wife so many years before.*

*Once inside, he mentally ran through the arrangements he
had given to his secretary. Next morning he would rise, then
head the Jaguar northwards out of dirty, noisy old London
and start a solitary week of walking in the Yorkshire Dales,
setting out each morning from the cottage he had bought
years ago. Then, his batteries fully recharged, a flight across
the Atlantic to deliver a big speech on the future of musical
education to an international Arts conference in Boston,
Massachusetts.*

Once again, the Hedfordshire County Youth Orchestra
had attracted a big audience. Nothing went wrong in the
Elgar; they were back on their toes and avoided the
snares of familiarity. Gwen's playing in the Shostakovich
was faultless as ever. The interval was a time of calm for
confident people who knew exactly what they were
doing.

After the interval, Liz got even more out of them than
ever. Something seemed to click in the Brahms; when it
was finished, Katie thought to herself: *that was perfect.
I'll never play anything as well as that again as long as I
live.*

But now there was more applause. Liz had left and
Hugo was striding to the platform.

*By mid-morning, the maroon Jaguar was on the M1 and
thrumming quietly northwards. While other motorists
listened to Radio 1 or shoved rock music cassettes into their*

*stereos, Gerald was listening to Stockhausen. He wondered
how many other drivers that morning shared his taste.*

*One o'clock. No motorway services for Gerald: he left the
M1 north of Nottingham and, leisurely and unhurried, made
his way to a hotel and country club he knew well.*

Katie wondered whether she only imagined a flustered
look on Hugo's face. There was nothing flustered or
indecisive about the way he brought them crashing into
the theme.

Katie had been dreading the first three variations. Last
night their subject had died – very nastily. But once the
lovely, nostalgic *Autumn* had begun, she felt happier.
This performance was a memorial to someone she never
knew except through the music. She felt peaceful,
content, as *To L.M.* wound its way to its end. When she
could, she watched Hugo to see if he was affected. No, he
was the involved, intent conductor, thinking – as far as
she could tell – only of his music.

*Gerald Swordblade had not watched television, listened to
the radio or even read a newspaper before he left London.
But as he sat in the hotel lounge reading* The Times *before
being called to his table, he turned to page 2 and his eyes
widened at the item in column three.*

MURDER OF PIANIST

Detectives in Hedford last night appealed for
information following the discovery of the body of 74-
year-old Laura Merchant, the concert pianist,
broadcaster and teacher. She had been shot through

the head and tied by the wrist to a jetty at the foot of the garden of her home by Cutler's Mere, Hedford. The discovery was made by her brother, 76-year-old George Merchant, author, broadcaster and traveller. Forensic experts believe the murder took place between 9.30 p.m. and 10.30 p.m. There were no signs of a break-in. Cutler's Mere is a well-known beauty spot attracting many visitors for sailing, lakeside and woodland walks and picnic areas.

Miss Merchant's fame as a pianist was based on her frequent recitals at the Wigmore and Queen Elizabeth Halls. She was a tireless champion of young composers and was also well known as an accompanist, especially of Schubert *Lieder*. For many years she taught at the Royal National Conservatoire of Music, where she trained as a student. (Obituary, page 6.)

Gerald Swordblade's eyes had widened almost into his hair by the time he finished reading. He put the paper down and for some minutes stared sightlessly out of the window. When a waiter came to him and said, "Your table is ready, sir," he picked up his paper, folded it neatly and followed him into the dining room. Here he ate a meal, not a mouthful of which did he taste.

Fourth variation. *Winter*. Bleak chords on the lower strings: rasping runs from the brass, metallic icicle tinkles from the woodwind. The winter Hugo envisaged was a permafrost: an unyielding, never-thawing season. Except that sudden storms, swirling blizzards, would sweep in on the brass and choking snowfall would smother the flutes and bassoons, leaving the icy foundations of the strings muted but never silent, always there in a persistent, creaking ground bass. Katie remembered Hugo saying there were monsters prowling. She could hear them; their shadowy footfalls pervaded this music, though perhaps their bones were now held frozen miles deep in the iron ground.

Gerald's journey was near its end. The Jaguar swooped round narrow roads in high, green and purple rocky country. The journey had been uneventful. Since leaving the last town, the only car he had seen was a white BMW parked in a layby just five miles from the cottage, as if its occupants had left it to ramble across the fells.

Would the cottage be stocked up? Would the refrigerator, the freezer, the wine racks, the drinks cupboard, be ready for his stay? Would Mrs Boothroyd from the farm have done the work for which he paid her, preparing for his visit? Of course she would. People here were dependable, could be trusted.

No wonder he came up here whenever he had a chance.

He locked the Jaguar up outside the stone-built cottage. He opened the front door. A fire was burning in the grate – a necessity even on this July day in such clear, fresh air and so high up. He smelt the spicy woodsmoke and his heart lightened. Yes, Mrs Boothroyd had done well. He would have his few precious days of blissful solitude.

Were there any messages? He ought to look. His number was ex-directory, so anyone ringing should have a purpose.

Yes, there was a message. He sat and listened to Gwen's voice.

"Hmm," he said musingly when she had finished.

He changed into walking clothes. His first venture would be a loosening ramble on the fell.

No sooner had he closed the front door behind him than the phone rang again. He did not go back to answer it.

On Granden Fell was a lightly scored piece. Katie had the impression of clear skies, fresh breezes, wide views. Sustained chords suggesting distance and long vistas alternated with subtle rhythms in which the original theme was very clear. Katie felt Hugo must love this place as much as G.S. did.

Gerald Swordblade returned invigorated. He had walked four miles and had seen no life except for sheep and curlews. Now he prepared himself a meal, took a bottle of white wine from the refrigerator and put on a Monteverdi CD. His holiday contentment was complete.

Next variation. *To G.S.* Now Katie had a notion of who G.S. might be. Throughout its duration, she could see the big-built but oddly dainty man in his expensive suit, with sleek silver hair and full, slightly reddened features. She tried to fit the music to what she had seen. This variation had a solid, four-square, dependable – almost comforting – treatment of the main theme. Katie knew that Hugo thought G.S. was *all right*. But the variations were in groups of three, so why should *Winter* be so disturbing and menacing? Its bleakness still echoed: things were not always what they seemed.

* * *

Gerald Swordblade sat in his armchair, lulled by wine, woodsmoke and music. Memories flooded, ghosts walked his mind, brought by the news of Laura's death and Gwen's message. Laura — so transparent, so good. What a terrible end to so gentle a life! Hugo — ah, the best pupil of all. And others. Alicia Vernon, one of Hugo's many conquests and one of the first he left high and dry. Alicia — forthright girl, admired by many, loathed by some. Pity she never really made it. Violinist with the Promenade Philharmonic — that didn't really fulfil her promise. Whose fault was that? Hugo's? His own? Fiona Tankerton, strong-willed and domineering. What a singer! Still thrilling them at Covent Garden, the Met, Bayreuth. Yes, she could belt out the Wagner — and had a fiery character to match. He was sad to receive that letter from her last year.

I'm giving it all up, Gerry. I'll retire at the top, before anyone can say I'm on the slide. Besides, there are so many other important things to do in life, aren't there?

Her leaving the opera stage would mark the end of an era.

And still the figures from the past stalked through his memory. William Weston — tall, sardonic, who ran the conducting course at the Conservatoire for a while but never quite made it himself. Frank — Hugo's contemporary and friend, liked, trustworthy, never quite one of the charmed inner circle. If only he'd had time to talk to Frank at Wardminster. He should have made time. But Hugo — yes, Hugo was, as always, the centre of everything. And memory of Hugo called up the memory of Ken Vanstone, the nearly man — nearly brilliant, nearly the best, nearly still alive to tell the tale. Thoughts of Ken made him think of Rosalie, his own wife, dead so long now. He shuddered. He tried never to remember that time. But he couldn't always blank it out. Not tonight, here, alone, warmed by wine and suffused by drowsy memories.

Yes, once they had sworn an oath to keep everlasting silence. Where was that bond now? Sir Gerald Swordblade, powerful, famous, talented and successful man, sat in his armchair and cried.

The last chords of the variation *To G.S.* died away. Katie rested her bow. The whole orchestra watched Hugo, waiting to be brought in for the next, *Spring*.

Gerald Swordblade had dozed. He woke suddenly. The fire was low. The CD had long since finished. The profound silence of hill, fell and dale enveloped the cottage.

Until something disturbed it. Suddenly alert, Gerald stood. He crossed to the window and peered into the darkness. He strained ears and eyes. Yes, there it was again.

He opened the front door and walked outside.

Hugo bowed. Katie watched him savour, then share his triumph as he motioned them to stand. The new-town dwellers of Byron Springs had enjoyed themselves and were showing it enthusiastically.

7

Next morning, Katie sought Gwen out after breakfast. Gwen had left Hugo to eat alone, his face
worried and tense. Dave was already in the foyer, going
through each newly delivered newspaper and carefully
refolding them so no enraged receptionist would insist he
bought them.

"Was there anything on the news this morning?" Katie
asked.

"No hint of any murder in Yorkshire," said Gwen. "If
someone's done anything to Gerald to follow a pattern,
no one's found him yet."

"Nothing in any paper," said Dave.

"So Laura Merchant's murder was just coincidence,"
said Katie.

"Don't be too sure just yet," said Gwen. "It's lonely
up there. You could be dead for months and nobody
would find you."

"Ring him up again," said Dave.

"What would I say?" said Gwen. " 'Sorry for bothering you, Gerry, but we just wanted to make sure you were still alive'?"

"At least we'll know he is," said Dave.

Gwen inserted money in the payphone and dialled the number.

"It's ringing," she said. She waited.

"No one's there," she said at last. "But the answering machine's switched off. So he's been in the cottage. He'll have got up early and gone off walking." But she didn't look happy.

"It doesn't prove anything," said Dave.

Loading up time came again. This time they were on the way to Hedford, their own county town. It would be strange for both Katie and Dave to spend a night in their home town but not in their own homes. The concert was in the Civic Hall and Katie's parents and Ricky would be in the audience. Katie would have a fleeting chat with them before a night in the dormitories of the one school in the county which took boarders, and then the journey down to London and the tour's finale.

Once again, Hugo drove off in the Porsche and Gwen stayed in the coach. Katie and Dave sat together.

"All right," said Dave. "What if he *has* been murdered? What if someone *is* going round killing the person the variation's dedicated to when it's being played? What would it all mean?"

"That there's someone around who's mad," said Katie.

"*And* very clever. *And* who knows a lot about Hugo and his variations. *And* about the way our tour's organized."

Katie was silent.

"Makes you think, doesn't it?" said Dave.

"Well, it couldn't have anything to do with Hugo himself," said Katie. "He's been with us every night, doing the conducting."

"I wonder where he goes to in the day," said Dave.

"Gwen said she thought he might have gone to the Royal National Conservatoire on Sunday," said Katie.

"I keep on hearing about that place," said Dave. "Hugo, Frank and Gwen all went there, this Swordblade bloke turns up and he's the Principal, some old girl who taught there gets bumped off. It never goes away."

"And then it turns out Sam's mum went there," mused Katie.

"She can't have anything to do with it," said Dave.

"No, but she was there when Hugo and Frank were students and Laura Merchant and Gerald Swordblade taught them."

"Why not ask Frank?"

"OK, ask him. I dare you."

Dave didn't answer. The thought of quizzing the County Music Adviser about his past didn't appeal.

"We'll ask Sam's mum," he said.

"*What* are we going to ask her?" said Katie.

"Let's think," said Dave. "These people were all there at the same time."

"But if the people in the variations are being killed, it's by someone who was there or knew about them and has a grudge."

"A long revenge?" suggested Dave.

"It must be for something very terrible," said Katie. "Or the murderer's a complete psychopath."

68

"And remember, this person knows all about the variations and when they're being played. There can't be many who do," said Dave.

"Frank, Liz and Hugo," said Katie.

"They're with us every night," said Dave.

"It could be someone close to Hugo," said Katie.

"Or Frank," said Dave.

"Why not Liz?" said Katie.

"No way," said Dave.

"I don't know anything about Liz," said Katie.

"Mrs Woolley to you," said Dave, sarcastically.

"She's divorced, isn't she?" said Katie.

"How should I know?" said Dave.

"I remember seeing a man waiting for her in a car after a rehearsal for the Christmas concert," said Katie. "Husband or boyfriend? I wonder."

"The programme says she didn't go to that Royal National place. She read music at university and then trained as a teacher," said Dave.

"But all the rest did," mused Katie. "Does something bind them together, I wonder? Something years old coming back to haunt them?"

"Find out at a cinema near you," said Dave.

"Don't be stupid," said Katie.

"But if Laura being murdered was just coincidence, then it's all stupid," said Dave. "And if this Swordblade man's all right and just gone walking…"

"We don't know that yet," said Katie.

The coaches arrived in Hedford. Everybody dumped luggage and sorted beds out. Then down to the canteen for lunch. They saw Sam's mum enter on her own and made sure no Friend of the Orchestra joined her before they could sit with her.

"You don't let go, do you?" she said when Katie asked if she thought the timing of Laura's murder had been anything more than very nasty coincidence. "No, I'm sure not. It's unthinkable."

"But just think it for a moment," persisted Dave.

"What are you saying?" said Mrs Belling.

"Well, perhaps something happened to her and Hugo," said Katie. "And perhaps Sir Thing as well. Gwen's dead worried because he's G.S. Someone's got something on them and is taking a revenge. Hugo's worried about *something*: Gwen says so. And Sir Whatsit turns up on Monday evening when Laura Merchant's being killed and Hugo wasn't pleased to see him."

"I'm not listening to this," said Mrs Belling, slicing into her pizza. "Your imaginations are running away with you. You'll get yourselves into trouble if you're not careful."

"But what if something happened to the Swordblade person last night?" said Dave. "He's probably G.S."

"But nothing did," said Mrs Belling.

"How do you know?" said Katie. "Gwen got no answer when she rang this morning. She said he must be out walking. What if he isn't?"

"If you feel this strongly, you should go to the police," said Mrs Belling.

"We might at that," said Dave.

Mrs Belling chewed silently. Then: "All right. There are some things which, now you mention it, come to mind. Remember, I didn't know Hugo all that well. He was in his final year when I was in my first. My trouble was we both left at the same time. But there were two really awful things that happened. Gerry Swordblade lost his wife Rosalie and two students ended up dead."

"Tell us more," said Dave.

"I remember Gerry and Rosalie had a cottage in the Cotswolds."

"He likes his holiday homes," said Katie.

"Not in the Cotswolds any more, he doesn't," said Mrs Belling grimly. "Rosalie was a lot younger than him: in her twenties when he was in his mid-forties. I fear she had an eye for young male students. She wasn't above taking them to the cottage when Gerry was away. Anyway, one of them, Julian – oh, God, this is terrible – was in the cottage with her one night when it caught fire. They must have been overcome by fumes. The cottage was miles from any town: by the time the Fire Brigades were there it was a complete inferno. The two had to be identified from dental records."

"This has put me off my pizza," said Dave.

"Anyway, the police suspected arson. But if it was, it was very clever; nothing could be proved. The obvious person to question was Gerry. The police had him in for hours, even though he was completely distraught. But his alibi was cast-iron: everybody vouched for where he was at the time."

"You mean Hugo, Laura, Frank..." said Dave.

"I can see what you're thinking," said Mrs Belling. "And, yes, now I come to think about it, you could well be right. Thought I'm not so sure about Frank. Hugo must have. And Alicia, his girlfriend at the time. Laura

71

Merchant did. And Bill Weston, he certainly did. Ken, probably. Fiona, definitely."

"Fiona?" said Kate.

"Fiona Tankerton, the opera singer."

"She's even more famous than Hugo," said Katie.

"And famous long before Hugo," said Mrs Belling. "I went to hear her at the ENO at the Coliseum last month. She's still brilliant."

"How come you remember all those names so quickly?" said Dave. "They were only Gerald Swordblade's alibi."

"Oh, they were much more than that," said Mrs Belling. "They were the inner ring, the charmed circle, the musical mafia, the group in the know, at the centre of everything. A knot of staff and students who gravitated round Gerald. He *spotted* them, I suppose you could say." Katie thought she detected bitterness in her voice. "They held music's future in their hands, or so they thought. Above the law, that's how they saw themselves."

Yes, there was bitterness there. And worse – strange after so long.

"You said two students died," said Dave. "I've only counted one."

"The other was Ken Vanstone," said Mrs Belling. "I remember he was Hugo's great friend. And Frank's too, now I come to think about it. Though I don't remember either Frank or Ken really being in Gerald's magic circle. Fringe figures, I suppose you could call them. They weren't marked out for great things like Hugo."

"What happened to Ken?" said Katie.

"Found dead in Regent's Park a month afterwards. He really *had* been murdered."

"Not by one of the magic circle?" said Dave.

"Oh, no. The police decided it was a mugging. He'd been stabbed; there was no wallet or money on him so he must have been set on and killed for whatever he was carrying. The police never got anybody for it. I remember Hugo and Frank being very upset and nobody going out alone for months afterwards."

Kate and Dave said nothing. They looked at each other, then back at Mrs Belling.

"So there you are," she said. "Terrible things happened that year, but they weren't connected. An accidental fire and a random killing for theft."

"And three people, who knew each other, all dead," said Dave.

"As big a coincidence as the timing of Laura Merchant's murder," said Katie.

"Of course it is. All coincidence," said Mrs Belling.

But her eyes betrayed her. These memories brought pain.

They had a surprise when they entered the Civic Hall that afternoon. Police cars were drawn up outside. Frank and Liz stood by the conductor's rostrum with two men, one in plain clothes, the other in the uniform of a police superintendent. As the orchestra members shuffled into their places, Frank spoke.

"Not to worry, folks. But the nice policemen here are just making a few enquiries. If you saw or spoke to Sir Gerald Swordblade on Monday night, they'd like to have a word."

"Working overtime," Dave muttered to Andy, the

second trombone. "They've already got a murder investigation here."

Katie, sitting next to Roger Curle at the first desk of the cellos, felt a sudden sinking feeling in her stomach. Something *must* have happened to Sir Gerald Swordblade. Then came another thought. If they were investigating his murder, had they realized it was linked with Laura Merchant's? Perhaps not. Whatever happened to Gerald Swordblade had been miles away and was being investigated by a different force. So probably no connection had been made – yet.

The police took over a dressing room for their interviews. As the rehearsal went distractedly on, Katie saw Gwen and Sam's mum go in and come out again; then she saw the two men sit at the back of the hall listening to the orchestra's stops and starts and Frank's now very muted instructions.

At 3.30, the main door opened suddenly. Hugo dashed in, not noticing the pair in the two seats close to where he entered.

"So sorry, everybody," he shouted breathlessly. "But for once I'm here to take my own rehearsal."

The superintendent rose. "Mr Hugo Malvern? Step this way, please."

Hugo went with them. Half an hour later he reappeared.

"I'm sorry," he called out to Frank. "I can't conduct this piece tonight. In fact, I never want to hear the cursed thing again."

8

There was a television set in the games room at the school. The item Katie and Dave half-expected came in the six o'clock news.

"Police are treating as suspicious the disappearance of the Principal of the Royal National Conservatoire of Music, Sir Gerald Swordblade, whose car was found abandoned this morning."

A picture came up of a large car being winched up from a narrow valley through which ran a foaming, rocky stream. Then came the face of a reporter.

"Sir Gerald, who owns a holiday cottage in North Yorkshire, was known to have arrived last night for a walking holiday. When a local farmer called with milk this morning, the house was empty."

Now came the ruddy, weatherbeaten face of the farmer.

"I wouldn't have thought owt about it, because he

often goes out early in t'morning. But this time his car were gone and all and he'd left front door open and t'light on in his living room. I thought that were right funny."

The reporter spoke again.

"Walkers found the car, a maroon Jaguar, in a beck some eight miles from the cottage at about mid-morning. Fears are growing for Sir Gerald's safety."

The reporter signed off. Katie and Dave looked at each other.

"We've got to do *something*," said Katie.

"The police?" said Dave.

"Not on our own. They wouldn't take us seriously."

"Then we have to get Gwen or Sam's mum."

Gwen was nowhere to be found. Mrs Belling was sitting in the staff common room with the other Friends of the Orchestra. She rose unwillingly when she saw them.

"All right," she said. "Tell the police what you suspect." She thought for a moment, then: "I'm coming with you." She turned to Arthur Armitage. "Arthur, tell Frank we're at the police station. Yes, I know we'll be cutting it fine, but I'll get these two back in time. Frank can hold me responsible if I don't."

The police station was a short distance away. As they walked, Mrs Belling said, "You tell them what you believe about the coincidences of the murders, but don't say anything about Hugo. I won't say a word about what I told you about Hugo and the magic circle. If I spoke out of turn here, we could all end up in deep trouble. But I want to know what happens."

Something's worrying her, thought Katie.

When they told the constable at the desk that they might have information about both Laura Merchant and Sir Gerald Swordblade, they were ushered into an interview room almost at once. A sergeant came in to take their statement.

Katie and Dave told their suspicions: the coincidence of Laura's death, Sir Gerald's disappearance and the playing of the variations; how someone called A.V. who lived near Carteret Woods in the North Downs should, at that rate, be very careful that night.

The sergeant listened, wrote everything down on a statement form, asked them to read it back and then both sign it. Then he at last made a comment, rather stiffly and formally.

"That is a line of enquiry we are aware of and are following up. We will relay your fears of a possible incident in the North Downs area to the local police. Thank you for your co-operation."

Soon, they were outside again.

"Is that it?" said Dave.

"Come on," said Mrs Belling. "I've got to get you to the hall in time for the concert."

Hugo meant what he said. He had refused to appear that night and nothing Frank could say would change his mind.

"If I could, I'd burn every copy there is. I wish I'd never thought of it. I wish you'd never asked me," he raved.

"But Hugo—" Frank started.

"Don't worry. I can't forbid you to play it. But I won't conduct it. I have things to do. I have to find Alicia."

This had been behind closed doors in the dressing room they shared at the Civic Hall. Hugo had burst out at that point, run to the car park and once again driven the Porsche away.

Gwen was quiet and listless.

"Yes, I've heard about Gerry," she said to Katie. "I don't know what to think any more. Who's going to be next?"

"A.V.," said Katie. "Who's A.V.?"

"I don't know," said Gwen. "But Hugo must have done something *very* terrible and now he's paying for it. It's as if writing the variations has unleashed the murders. I wish I knew more about him. But he just clams up when I ask him about his student days."

A memory stirred in Katie's mind.

"Gwen, do you think that's what the man you saw in Leeds meant by, 'Now he's given him the key'?"

Gwen looked at her for a moment.

"You're right," she said at last. "You must be. This Ken person, that's who the murderer must be. Ken was going to see Hugo again. That's what the man said."

"Who's Ken?" said Dave.

"Not a clue," said Gwen.

"There's only one Ken that I know of," said Katie. "The Ken Sam's mum told us about. Ken Vanstone. But he's dead."

"But Hugo *can't* have anything to do with the murders. All he did was to write a piece of music."

There was relief in her voice which Dave broke at once.

"Sorry," he said. "That doesn't add up. If Hugo's variations are a sort of signal to start things going, then he must have meant them to be. I don't believe some murderer was waiting there saying, 'I'll start the killing the very moment someone writes Theme and Variations describing all the victims.'"

"What are you saying?" said Gwen.

"If there's a murder plot, Hugo's *got* to be in it. It's obvious."

Tears started in Gwen's eyes. "I don't believe you," she said.

Katie came to her aid.

"But why should he do something which would draw such attention to himself?" she said.

They all three looked at each other.

"It's impenetrable," said Gwen.

Before the concert started, Frank announced that, owing to sudden indisposition, Hugo was unable to conduct Variations on a Folk Song Theme that evening: Liz Woolley would be an effective substitute. There was a buzz of disappointment, then sympathetic applause.

The concert went smoothly enough. Gwen appeared looking calm and composed. Her playing was less flowing than usual: there was tension in her hands. But the piece ended efficiently enough and as always her reception was enormous.

She stood accepting the applause. A Friend of the Orchestra appeared from the side of the stage with a bouquet. She accepted it smilingly, then Katie saw her stiffen suddenly and the smile fade from her face. She nearly dropped the bouquet as she stared at the audience. Then she seemed to collect herself, smile again and walk off the platform for the last time.

During the interval, she came to Katie.

"That man's there," she whispered. "Sitting in the fourth row."

"What man?" said Katie.

"The one I met in Leeds who gave me the message for Hugo. The little man with the moustache. What's he doing here?"

"He's a fan," said Katie. "He follows you around."

Gwen didn't seem pleased with this remark.

"I can do without fans like that," she said. "He's creepy."

"Let's ask him after the concert," said Katie. "Perhaps he's got another message for you."

"I'll think about it," said Gwen doubtfully. "Watch out for him. End seat on the left, fourth row."

When they returned to their places, Katie looked to where Gwen had said. Yes, there he was – small, rather weaselly, with a toothbrush moustache, shiny black hair plastered back over his head and wearing a very smart and well-cut blue pin-stripe suit.

No time to look any more. Liz was at the rostrum, baton raised. They began the Brahms.

As he drove, Hugo was torn between going as fast as he dared and driving unobtrusively so that no police car would stop, fine and – worst of all on this particular night – delay him.

Taking the M25 eastbound over the Dartford Crossing would be the best way to reach Alicia's house near Carteret Woods.

"Don't worry, Alicia!" he shouted to the air as he drove. "I behaved badly to you once. I went when you wanted me to stay. But now I'm coming to protect you."

Liz took her usual applause for a job well done. Brahms had been effectively dealt with yet again. Now the audience coughed, shifted, whispered, expectantly but disappointedly. No Hugo. As much as anything else, that was who they had come to see.

The hall resounded again with the sounds of tuning up. Once Katie was satisfied with her cello, she looked out at the audience, to where the man with the moustache was sitting. Now she could study him more deeply. A sharp, rather pale face, small eyes, and that little moustache and the flat shiny hair. Katie sometimes studied people's faces and thought: Why do they *want* to look like that? She felt this now – the man in the fourth row seemed to have gone out of his way to look shifty and mean.

No more time for speculation. Liz was waiting, the clapping sounded round the hall and Hugo's variations started.

Hugo had left the M25. He drove along a narrow road which cut through wooded countryside. In the gathering dusk, the yellow of primroses and the carpet of bluebells could still be seen under the spreading branches. Alicia lived near here: her house was on the edge of the village the other side of Carteret Woods. She wasn't Alicia Vernon any more: she had married three years after leaving the Conservatoire. But that had ended, rather sadly. Alicia had come back to live in her parents' house. When they died it was hers — a convenient base for a musician's life.

How could he forget Alicia? Small, stocky, strong: you'd think she was an athlete — a shot putter or javelin thrower — and not the very fine violinist she actually was. She had dominated a large part of his life when they were students. Alicia had thought — he knew this for a fact — that they would stay together afterwards. He knew how he had hurt her and how angry she was. But time heals all wounds — doesn't it? — and part of him had never forgotten Alicia. Perhaps he could now perform her a great service. It was all she deserved.

Katie found getting through the theme and the first six variations a trial. She had to close her mind to all the associations they now possessed and think only of how to play the notes. When the final chord of *To G.S.* died away she felt almost as if she was starting a completely new work. *Summer, In Carteret Woods, To A.V.* Well, no one seemed to have any idea of who A.V. could be. This made her feel better. Her mood lightened as the first chords of *Summer* started.

The Porsche came down the village street. Dusk had descended. Where was Alicia's house? Hugo had not been there for years and there had been new building. He had to stop and think. Yes, that turning on the right. Up there, at the end of the lane, set back behind a lawn with trees at the rear. That was it. He signalled right and drove slowly up the lane.

* * *

Summer was a happy, lyrical piece. Strings, woodwind – especially the flutes – and the trumpets with their high, bright, golden tone, dominated the start. There was hope in the affirmative chords, the jaunty rhythmic figures. Then the mood changed to a long violin solo which Samantha always managed beautifully: soulful, lush, turning the original taut tune of *Little Musgrave* into a leaping, swooning, romantic melody. Katie wondered if this solo was a tribute: did A.V. play the violin? Hugo was not, she felt, just expressing a season of the year. He was remembering a season in his own life. Katie was sure about this because as she grew to know the variation she recognized it as expressing something in her life as well.

This was it. A low brick wall topped by small fir trees, a wrought-iron gate. Hugo remembered this sight from years ago with painful clarity. He stopped the car, switched the lights off, got out and locked it. The "beep" of the remote control seemed so loud and the sudden yellow hazard lights so bright in the dusk that Hugo thought he must rouse the whole village.

He walked up to the darkened house. There was a light on upstairs. At he watched, it went out. Another light came on downstairs. He approached the front door. Without warning he was bathed in hard brightness as security lights automatically came on.

In Carteret Woods carried on the mood of *Spring*. Katie could see soft, flowery ground under trees, shafts of sunlight through branches and leaves in complicated tracery, could know the solid, comforting trunks of oak and ash, sycamore and cypress. Yes. *In Carteret Woods* was a magical place and Hugo, as well as A.V., loved it.

Hugo rang the bell. No answer. But the downstairs light stayed on. Why didn't whoever was in there come to the door?

Then he realized. The house was empty. The lights were all on time switches. Alicia had obviously become very security-conscious.

Relief swept over him. If Alicia was away, no one could murder her in Carteret Woods tonight.

Suddenly there was movement behind him. A man's voice spoke.

"I think you'd better come with us, sir."

Hugo turned. Two policemen were looking at him. One was speaking into his radio. They did not seem friendly.

A.V. was a person Katie might have liked. The violin solo of *Summer* appeared again – a different key and a different rhythm – but Samantha managed it just as well. The repetition, the reference between *Summer* and *To A.V.* gave no notion that Hugo had run out of ideas. A.V. and summer were inextricably linked in Hugo's mind. And A.V. was definitely a woman. Her bow raised ready for the next cello entry, Katie listened to Samantha's solo, marvelled at its smoothness, its singing, its lovely clarity of line. But behind it, she could tell, was yearning and regret.

The Promenade Philharmonic Orchestra of London was not

in its usual home in the concert hall of the Citadel Arts Centre. Their tour of Belgium, Holland, Denmark and northern Germany was nearly over, ending with a sell-out concert in the Concertgebouw Hall in Amsterdam, under the chief conductor, the Russian Sergei Sholokhov.

As they played, though, everyone on the platform was worried. One of their number had, that morning, disappeared from her hotel room. The violins were playing one member short. There would be difficulties now about leaving for England. The British Consul had been called in and the Embassy alerted. Tomorrow, if she didn't turn up, their departure would be delayed – which would be terrible. They all wanted their summer break, and there would be protracted difficulties with the Dutch police.

Nobody could know that the body of Alicia Stokes (née Vernon) was at the bottom of one of Amsterdam's many canals and that it would not be found until the person who had weighted it down with stones and tipped it quietly over a bridge saw fit to tell where it was.

The variations were over. Liz stood and so did the orchestra to accept the audience's applause.

Katie looked to see how the man with the moustache had enjoyed it. But his seat was empty. He had left early.

9

"Gwen, did you see that man again?" said Katie. "No. Why should I?" Gwen replied.

They were back in the school after the concert. There had been a little party: parents and friends had gathered to meet the orchestra over coffee and biscuits. Katie had exchanged a few words with her parents and Ricky, saying nothing about what most concerned her. Only now they were gone did she manage to see Gwen.

"I thought he might give you another message."

"If he came near me I'd run a mile," Gwen answered.

"But he must be here for some reason. He's not an orchestra groupie," said Katie. "Perhaps he left a message for somebody else."

"I don't want to think about him," said Gwen.

"Who could it be?" said Katie to herself.

Hugo was both angry and puzzled. He had been taken to

the local police station and questioned by an inspector and a detective constable. It had been very uncomfortable.

"Why were you here, sir?"

"Why were you trying to enter a house which is not yours?"

"I keep telling you. I knew Miss Vernon years ago. I called on her. She was out. What's criminal about that?"

"Why did you come *tonight*, sir?"

"Why *not* tonight? Look, I'm Hugo Malvern. Anyone in music would vouch for me; you must have seen me on BBC2 and Channel 4..."

"What if we were to tell you that we received information from another police force that an attempt might be made tonight on the life of a certain person whom we identified as Mrs Stokes?"

"Mrs Stokes?"

"Miss Vernon was married, sir."

"Yes, I know. But that's impossible. How could you know...?"

"You were questioned today by the Hedfordshire Police."

"Not about this. Alicia's name was never mentioned."

"Yet you came rushing straight here."

"Look," said Hugo. He told them about the variations, the coincidences of Laura's murder and Gerald's disappearance and his fear that Alicia might go the same way.

"I don't think I'd want to be a friend of yours, sir," said the detective constable.

"Why didn't you say all that before?" said the inspector.

"I wish I had."

"And now you can set your mind at rest," said the inspector. "Mrs Stokes is not in the village. She is on tour with a symphony orchestra, surrounded all day by hundreds of people in the biggest cities in Europe. What could be safer?"

"Thank God for that," said Hugo. "Can I go now?"

"Indeed you can, sir. But watch your step in future."

Hugo rose and left without another word. His car had been brought to the police station, and he drove off without a backward look. He was still shaking from his second police interview in one day, but he was also relieved that Alicia had not been at home. It really seemed as if, after all, there might not be a fatal succession night after night let loose by his own thoughtless over-ingenuity. Oh, the whole enterprise had been stupid. He should have realized, he should have thought a bit more...

The Porsche was approaching the motorway. Which way now?

Why, west of course. Then turn off on to the M23, past Gatwick Airport and into the Sussex lanes to his own secluded house set in woodland. He'd have one comfortable night at least. Then up early next morning and into London. An awful suspicion was forming in his mind about the last concert and the final variation. He must let Frank know he would be back – and at all costs he had to be in the Citadel Centre on Friday to conduct.

If Hugo had been more experienced in such things, he would have noticed that, among all the headlights keeping pace with him as he raced along the motorway, one pair had stayed behind him ever since he had left Alicia's village. They were still behind him as he turned off the motorway and they dogged his progress along the roads to his house until, as he swung into his drive and got out to unlock his garage, they were extinguished. The white BMW they were part of stood by the grass verge in darkness. The driver sat quietly, pondering the next move.

After breakfast next morning, Katie and Dave found themselves in an uncomfortable interview. Mrs Belling, looking flustered, came up to Katie and said, "Frank wants to see you both. Now. It's about going to the police. I warn you, he's furious."

Frank was waiting in the room which, during term-time, was used by the member of staff on duty. Liz was with him. Frank looked rumpled in an old green sweater and grey trousers, Liz trim in blouse and faded blue jeans. They both looked stern.

"Mrs Belling tells me," Frank said, "that you and she visited the police last night. May I ask why?"

The politeness, they knew from the unfriendliness of his eyes, was deceptive.

Haltingly, they recounted everything. Frank and Liz listened without a word. When they had finished, Liz spoke.

"Don't you think you've both been very silly?" she said. "It sounds far-fetched rubbish to me. And if there *is* a connection between our concerts and these other events, at best you're involving people who are completely innocent and getting them, us and yourselves into needless trouble; at worst, you're putting yourselves in danger."

Frank took up where Liz left off.

"I was very angry when Mrs Belling told me – as she had to. I nearly sent you both home there and then. I've calmed down now. You can stay. But just be careful. There's to be *no more* of this. Keep out of what doesn't concern you. Now get out and get ready."

Outside in the corridor they looked at each other.

"Well, that's it, then," said Katie.

"Oh, no, it isn't," said Dave. "Doesn't Frank realize he's probably next?"

The coaches were loaded; everyone was off to London and the vast and sprawling Citadel Arts Centre, home of the Royal Classic Theatre Company and the Promenade Philharmonic Orchestra of London. As the coaches bowled south down the motorway, a feeling spread that the puny stuff was over: now they were really in the big time.

They would stay two nights in a University Hall of Residence close to the Citadel Centre and just down the road from the Royal National Conservatoire. They would have two afternoons of rehearsal in the state-of-the-art concert hall where most of the great orchestras of the world had played, and on Thursday evening they would all see the Royal Classic Theatre's new *Hamlet*. The rest of their time in London was free. After the last concert it was traditional to have a final get-together. Frank had arranged a gigantic curry supper to round everything off. It would all be great.

Or, for Katie and Dave, it *should* have been great. But there was now too much to think about. They sat together four seats from the back of the coach, quiet, glum and chastened. Frank's warning had hurt. Behind them were gathered the more raucous members of the brass and percussion who, not for the first time on the coach, were singing.

Their choice of songs had not always been to the taste of Frank and Liz. Several times Frank had shot them dirty looks and sometimes he had come to the back of the coach. When he returned to his seat he would mutter to Liz, "Remind me never to audition anyone in future who confesses to playing rugby."

On this journey, though, they had at last realized that *Little Musgrave* itself was worth singing. After all, the words were printed in the concert programme and the tune was capable of providing a good belting shout in the back seat of a coach just as well as food for Hugo's elaborate musical musings.

Their rendition had lasted for miles, interspersed with loud laughter. Now they had come to the verse they liked best.

> "Get up! Get up! Little Musgrave,
> And put your trousers on.
> For it will not be said throughout the land
> That I killed a naked man."

The verse ended with a huge cheer – and a remark from Dave that sent thoughts scurrying through Katie's mind.

"I wonder why Hugo chose *Little Musgrave*?"

"He liked the tune," she replied.

"There's plenty of other tunes just as good. And very similar. Folk songs don't vary that much."

"Perhaps he liked the words as well," said Katie.

"That's what I was thinking," said Dave.

They were silent as the crew behind them shouted out the death of Lady Barnard. Then Katie said slowly, "I wish Frank hadn't told us to keep out of this. I've just had a thought."

"Who said we were going to?" said Dave. "Tell me."

"Hugo dedicating the variations to people seems to be a signal to a murderer. You don't think the story of Little Musgrave is another signal?"

"Why not?" said Dave. "Let's think about it."

He found a crumpled copy of the concert programme in his holdall. He smoothed it out at the page where a version of *Little Musgrave* was printed.

"It says here there are lots of versions. Hugo put this one together, taking the best bits from each," said Dave.

"Then this is what he *wanted* people to see," said Katie.

They read it together silently. Then Dave said, "Let's see if we've got the story right. Little Musgrave must be one of Lord Barnard's knights. Lady Barnard fancies him and asks him to go off with her."

"And Musgrave says he will," continued Katie, "but Lady Barnard's page overhears. He thinks his duty's more to his lord than the lady so he runs off and tells him."

"Lord Barnard says if it's true, the page can have anything he wants, but if it's a lie, he'll be hanged," said

Dave. "Then he gets all his men to break in on Lady Barnard and Little Musgrave."

"So there they are, creeping in to where the two are sleeping," Katie went on. "Little Musgrave hears noises outside, Lady Barnard says it's nothing. Then the men burst in."

"Was the page with them?" said Dave.

"It doesn't say," said Katie. "Is that important?"

"It could be," said Dave.

"Lord Barnard tells Little Musgrave to get up and put his clothes on because he won't kill a naked man. They fight. Musgrave is killed. Lord Barnard kills his wife," said Katie.

"And Lord Barnard has them buried together but with Lady Barnard on top because she was nobly born. And that's it," said Dave.

"So why did Hugo go out of his way to choose it?' said Katie. "And does it have anything to do with the murders?"

"What did Sam's mum tell us yesterday?" said Katie. "About how Hugo and Gerald and Laura Merchant were in the magic circle?"

"Well, that there were those three and that opera singer woman…"

"Fiona Tankerton?"

"That's her. And two others. I forget their names.

"Alicia something," said Katie. "Hugo's girlfriend. Sam's mum never said her surname. And someone called Weston."

"That's six," said Dave. "What about the one who got murdered? Ken Vanstone."

"The mysterious Ken," said Katie. "But he was just mugged in the park; his murder can't be to do with this."

"That's not all Mrs Belling told us," said Dave.

"You mean about Gerald's wife?" said Katie. "Killed in a fire at their weekend cottage. Rosalie, that was her name."

"Yes, and *who was she with*?" said Dave triumphantly.

"You're right," said Katie. "A student. What was he called? Julian. Sam's mum never said a surname."

"*Julian Something equals Little Musgrave.*" Dave's eyes lit up with the perfection of the insight.

"What are you saying? That Rosalie was Lady Barnard? That means Gerald Swordblade was Lord Barnard. And that must mean—"

"That the house burning down *wasn't* an accident. Gerald killed them and then set fire to it himself. Hugo knows. And he's written this piece to *tell* him he knows."

"That's running on a bit fast," said Katie.

"It fits," said Dave.

"So what about the page?" said Katie.

Dave thought for a moment. Then: "Obvious, Ken Vanstone. He found out and told Gerald."

"And got murdered for his pains?" said Katie.

"Could be," said Dave.

"But that's wrong," said Katie. "Lord Barnard says if the page is right, he'll get all the lands he wants. If he's wrong, he'll be hanged. Well, Ken was right. But he ended up dead."

"You've heard about shooting the messenger," said Dave.

"But Ken's murder was just a random mugging."

"With all that's going on, is that likely?" said Dave.

"So Sir Gerald Swordblade did three murders when Hugo was a student?"

"Looks like it."

Katie thought again.

"It doesn't add up," she said. "He's disappeared. He's quite likely dead now. But he's not the only one. What about Laura Merchant? What did she have to do with it? Who's A.V?"

"Alicia?"

"Could be. But we don't know her surname," said Katie. "And what about F.T?"

"Frank Thurlow, obviously. Which is why he should listen to what we say, not threaten to kick us out."

"Or Fiona Tankerton. But what have *they* got to do with it – besides being in the magic circle? And what about Hugo? *Why* should he bring all this up now? Is he involved? Is someone going to have a go at him?"

Dave was musing. "They were all the people who gave Gerald his alibi. Perhaps that's why they're being got rid of."

"So it's someone who was close to Rosalie," said Katie.

"Or to this Julian bloke who got fried with her," said Dave.

The coach was approaching London's northern suburbs. Soon it would come off the motorway. Katie looked out of the window.

"It doesn't *really* fit," she said. "I still don't see *why* Ken Vanstone should have been murdered. And I don't see why Hugo has done all this now, after so many years."

"Neither do I," said Dave. "And perhaps it's not all a

perfect fit. But I bet you we're on the right track."

They had followed the usual routine. The coach dropped them at the Hall of Residence to dump luggage, sort out rooms and have a quick lunch. Then they went to the Citadel Centre to rehearse.

In the concert hall they looked about in wonder at the raked seating, the tiered galleries, the restful fawn, white and grey colour scheme. They spoke in hushed whispers, testing the sharp acoustic where sounds were exact and crystal clear. They tuned up and suddenly their instruments sounded much better than they had ever known them before.

Then they sat back, waiting for Frank and Liz to appear, feeling that they had really arrived.

10

"First things," said Frank. "Hugo *will* be here tomorrow. There was a message waiting here for me. He's very sorry; a lot's happened. But he wouldn't miss the final concert for anything. Second thing: I know that some of you have been a bit upset about the police interrupting us and some fantastic rumours going around about murders being connected with our concerts." He studiously averted his eyes from Katie and Dave as he said this. "Well, I'll say one thing and let that be an end of it. Nobody need worry. This business has *nothing* to do with us or with Hugo or with anyone else connected with the orchestra. The police have been following up a few leads which seemed to point our way, and they've sorted them. It's all coincidence, so forget it. *Nothing* must spoil this tour. OK?"

"OK," everyone said. A few in the orchestra plainly

didn't have a clue what he was talking about.

"Now, let's *do* this," he said. "And when we've sorted out last night's fluffs and got used to this magnificent hall, then your time's your own until seven-fifteen this evening, when you're all to be outside the box office of the theatre for the *Hamlet* performance. There you'll be accounted for by me, Liz or a Friend of the Orchestra and given your ticket. Tomorrow you've a free morning until lunchtime and then I want you all here, smart as paint, at two-thirty, ready for a final run-through. Now, let's play."

So they played, and the glorious sounds were even clearer, more magical than ever, in this perfectly designed, purpose-built space for music.

They were out by three. There was a lot to see. The Citadel Centre itself would take days to explore fully. It was a huge complex on many levels; the concert hall and the main theatre both opened out into a vast indoor foyer of bars and bookshops, like a shopping mall. On other levels were art galleries, exhibition spaces, meeting rooms, recital rooms, and rehearsal space, leading to the Palm Court full of exotic indoor plants and, at the very top, a big roof garden. Outside, fountains played into artificial lakes and walkways stretched past luxury flats to the outside world and – right next door – the Royal National Conservatoire of Music.

"Can't lose that place, can we?" said Dave.

For once, Katie and Dave weren't on their own. Samantha and Roger were with them. They drank coffee at a table outside the main complex, watching the fountains play in the warm afternoon sunshine. They were planning how to use the afternoon.

The tables round them were full. There had been a university degree-awarding ceremony going on: everywhere people wearing gowns and hoods, holding scrolls and with broadly grinning faces, were being photographed by admiring parents and friends. The four from the orchestra wondered if they would be doing the same not many years hence and whether it would be worth it.

Suddenly Katie gripped Dave's arm.

"*Look!*" she cried.

"What at?" said Dave, slightly irritated. He had been deep in conversation with Roger.

"It's him again," said Katie. "The man with the moustache."

"Rubbish," said Dave, not even looking. "Millions of men have moustaches."

"It *is*. What's he doing here? Why is he following us?"

Dave now looked up. He saw Katie was right.

"Following Gwen, more like," he said.

"You two are getting obsessed by this," said Samantha. "Frank's right. Leave it to the police."

The man got up and left. Katie suddenly made up her mind.

"I'm following him," she said.

She was gone, dodging past people snapping and being snapped, to where she last saw the small hurrying figure. He was now wearing light fawn slacks and a dark green polo shirt. She kept sight of him all the way along the walkway to the Citadel Centre's main entrance. Across the road was an underground station. She watched him look both ways before he crossed a road thick with taxis and cars to the ticket machines on its main concourse. She crossed the road as well and stood watching him, trying to see where his ticket was for. Then he turned slowly and looked deliberately at her.

His was not an attractive face. The flat hair did not gleam much now. The little moustache was the same, but round it was dark, unshaven stubble. Little eyes gleamed piggily. His look said, *I knew you were following me. And I know who you are.*

Then he stuffed pound coins in the machine, took out a travelcard and disappeared with this passport to the whole system until midnight, leaving Katie none the wiser.

"Satisfied?" said a voice behind her.

She turned. Dave had been following as well.

"No," she said. "I wanted to see where he's going."

"And did you?"

"No chance. I can't follow him. He bought a travelcard. He could go anywhere. There's three separate lines meeting here."

Dave thought for a minute.

"Why should you want to follow him?" he said.

"Because he started all this. He brought the message to Gwen in the first place. He's *in* it."

"All right," said Dave. "You've convinced me. We could try. If we get travelcards, we can go anywhere as well. And if we lose him, we can still have a good wander round London."

So they did. They stuffed coins into the machine, took their cards and change and rushed towards the trains.

The first platforms were for the Metropolitan and Circle lines. They were lucky at once.

"There he is," squealed Katie. "On the opposite platform."

They dashed over the bridge and took up cautious positions behind but not close to the man.

He did not appear to have seen them. The platform was crowded for mid-afternoon. The indicator said CIRCLE LINE TRAIN APPROACHING. With a rumble and a squeal the coaches drew to a halt. Katie and Dave saw the moustached man slip through the sliding doors and take a seat by the window. They got into the next carriage and stood by the doors, even though the train was barely two-thirds full. They needed to survey every stop. The train proceeded round its great circle: Moorgate, Liverpool Street, Bank, Tower Hill, to Westminster, St James's Park, Victoria and Sloane Square. At each stop they leaned out as the doors opened, but he never emerged.

Until South Kensington.

"There he goes," said Dave.

Again, they tried to keep him in view. Once through the ticket barriers, they realized he was not going to disappear into the crowded street; instead he made for the foot tunnel which led to the Museums. This was awkward. How could they not be seen and heard unless the tunnel was packed with people?

And, of course, it was not. Lined with dingy tiles, it stretched, dim, echoing and empty, in front of them.

The man never turned round.

"He's got no idea we're after him," Dave muttered.

Katie was not so sure. She had a feeling that it was more a case of *not caring* that they were after him.

The tunnel seemed unbearably long. No exits appeared to interest him. Katie was beginning to think he would walk its entire length simply because he had an aversion to the open air, when he suddenly disappeared.

"He's going to the Science Museum," she whispered.

"Only for a cup of tea, I hope," said Dave. "It costs a bomb to go in there."

His hopes were dashed. By the time they entered the museum they saw the man was paying to go through the turnstiles.

"What do we do?" said Katie.

"Split up. One follows, the other stays here watching."

"That's no good. The one staying here will see him come out but won't be able to follow if the one who goes in has lost him and is still looking. We'll have to go together."

"What if he's just come to look round the exhibits?"

"Is it likely? I bet he's arranged to meet someone here."

"OK. We'll both go," said Dave. "To hell with the cost."

The man had already disappeared. They searched every gallery, passing vast stationary steam engines and huge early turbines; upstairs to where lifelike patients underwent primitive surgery for ever poised in mid-incision; higher still and higher to where all was quiet, hushed and less spectacular. Crude but ingenious attempts to harness electricity were trapped in glass cases.

Here they saw him. Katie was right: he was deep in conversation. They could see his back view. At first, Katie thought he was talking to himself or into a tape recorder. But he gestured with his hands and then was still: he had a companion obscured by an exhibition case.

"This is maddening," muttered Dave.

They crouched behind another exhibition case, not daring to move. They listened hard, but whatever was said merged into the general background babble of the museum.

After five minutes, they realized the man had moved out of their sight. They watched and waited, then they heard footsteps down the far side of the gallery. They stared towards where the footsteps came from. Then they caught a glimpse of the man and with it another form seen too fleetingly to make much of except for a flash of something light blue.

"I think it's a woman," whispered Dave.

"Now what do we do?" Katie hissed.

"They're leaving the gallery. They *must* be going downstairs."

"They've split – one in the lift, the other on the stairs."

"Well, we'd better stick together."

Downstairs again, standing where they could see across the main entrance foyer, they searched the crowd.

"There he is," said Katie.

The green shirt and fawn slacks stood out against other clothes as he made for the main exit.

"He's on his own again," said Dave.

"But whoever he was with wore light blue," said Katie.

"Look," said Dave.

It was a warm day and light blue seemed colour of the month. Light blue skirts, shirts, washed-out jeans – the Science Museum seemed to be a celebration of the sky. Their quarry's dark green shirt looked like an unexpected island in an ocean.

"Off we go again," said Dave.

"Will he go back down the tunnel?" said Katie.

He did. Once again down the echoing passage, then into South Kensington station – and again they found themselves skulking at the back of the platform, watching him waiting at the front.

An eastbound Circle Line train came in, fuller this time. Rush hour was nearly here.

"We daren't lose him," said Dave. "We'll have to risk the same carriage."

Once again they stood, so they could see the back of his head where he sat close to a door. They settled for a long journey.

It was not to be. Two stops later, at Victoria, the man suddenly got up – as if, Katie thought, on impulse.

"Come on," she said.

The doors opened; the man was through. Katie and Dave, hand in hand, pushed their way past milling people, saw him follow the WAY OUT AND VICTORIA LINE sign and watched the back of his head as he stood on the escalator going down. He made for the northbound platform.

The platform was crowded. The man worked his way towards the edge. They realized there was no chance any more of observing unseen from further back – there were just too many people and too big a chance of not being able to get on the train he boarded. So they worked their way to the edge as well until they were standing about six metres from where they had last seen him.

The indicator said FIRST TRAIN WALTHAM-STOW 1 MINUTE.

They waited.

"I can't see him," Dave muttered.

The indicator changed. TRAIN APPROACHING.

They heard its rumble and saw bright lights in the tunnel.

"Where is he?" Dave said in sudden alarm.

The train was now banging along the edge of the platform.

Suddenly, Katie felt a strong weight on her shoulder pushing her off balance. The train's noise was very loud. She staggered. The edge of the platform seemed to rise up to hit her. Below it she saw, with split-second painful clarity, blackness edged with shining rail, and she realized that nothing was going to stop her falling on to it as the train roared deafeningly over her.

Down she went, in free fall.

"*Katie!*" She heard a howl of horror, then strong arms looped round her. For an appalling second she thought gravity would take both herself and their owner to their deaths, then their strength prevailed and she was dragged back as the train passed by not six inches from her head. She found herself sprawling on the platform with Dave, sprawling with her, looking in her face.

Concerned people gathered round, looking on.

"What happened? Did she faint?" said someone.

"Faint?" said Dave, looking up at them. "Not my Katie. She was pushed. And I know who pushed her. Come on."

He yanked Katie to her feet and dragged her away.

"The rat!" he shouted. "I'll kill him!"

"He's on the train," gasped the badly shaken Katie.

"Is he heck," replied Dave. "He's off the platform. We're not letting him go. Not now. He's known we've been after him all the time. He tried to murder you. We're on to something *big*!"

11

But they had lost him. He was swallowed up in the crowds.

"I want to sit down," said Katie. She and Dave left the Underground station and went with the flow to the main line terminus. Here, under the vast glazed roof and on the crowded concourse, they made for the eateries on the Victoria Plaza. Dave bought two coffees and they found a table.

"Are you all right?" said Dave.

The shock was just beginning to take effect.

"He tried to murder me," Katie said. She sipped her coffee. Now she really *did* feel faint.

"So this man's capable of that," said Dave. "He must be deep in this, whoever he is. But he can't have *done* the murders."

"Why not?" said Katie. She was trying hard to think constructively. If she gave way to wallowing in fright, she would be of no use to anyone. "He could have murdered Laura Merchant; he could have been in Yorkshire when Sir Gerald Swordblade disappeared."

"But he was at the concert last night," said Dave.

"There was no murder last night," replied Katie. "The sequence didn't work."

"True," said Dave.

Then Katie noticed a man at a nearby table reading the *Evening Standard*. A headline caught her eye: *BRITISH VIOLINIST MISSING IN AMSTERDAM*. A very weird thought flashed across her mind.

"Stay here," she said. "I'm buying a paper."

She was back quickly and spread the front page out over the table. They found the headline and read.

Police in Amsterdam are investigating the disappearance of Alicia Vernon, a violinist with the Promenade Philharmonic Orchestra of London which is just completing a European tour. Miss Vernon — formerly married to merchant banker Maximilian Stokes — was last seen in the orchestra's hotel at nine o'clock when she told colleagues she would be away for an hour or so to have coffee with an old friend. One orchestra colleague said, "Alicia seemed quite excited. She said she had been rung up by 'a real voice from the past'." Concern grew when Miss Vernon did not arrive for afternoon rehearsal or for the final sell-out concert of the tour in the world-famous Concertgebouw Hall.

The rest of the orchestra arrives home today. From their headquarters at the Citadel Centre, the orchestra's managing director said this morning...

Katie did not read on. She just stared aghast at the paper.

"It's A.V." she said. "Alicia Vernon. The sequence *did* work!"

"I never knew Carteret Woods were in Amsterdam," said Dave.

"They don't have to be," Katie replied. "If you're going to murder someone at a particular time, it has to be where they are, not where the music says they'd like to be."

"We don't know she's dead," said Dave.

"Of *course* she's dead. I know deep down she's dead." Katie's voice was anguished. "Dave, what are we going to do?"

She almost fell towards him and pushed her face on to his shoulder. He put his arm round her and they clung to each other silently while the crowds milled round Victoria station, dashed up to the Plaza, ate, drank and rushed on again.

"I'm scared," Katie muttered. "This has been a game so far. Like *Cluedo*: solving a mystery that's got nothing to do with us."

"I thought you wanted to solve it to protect Hugo because you fancied him," said Dave.

"Oh, Dave, not *really*. From afar, perhaps. I fancy Tom Cruise as well. But this mystery was like watching people on a TV screen – like an interactive game. Now we're *in* it."

Dave was silent.

"There's *someone*," said Katie. "This someone knows when and where we do things. This someone can be in

Hedford, Yorkshire, Amsterdam – wherever the victims are when we play Hugo's variations—"

"– and here, trying to push you under a train?" Dave interrupted.

"But that can't be," said Katie. "Like you said, he was in Hedford last night. He can't be in two places at once."

"You can't be sure anyone was killed last night," said Dave.

"Yes, I can," said Katie firmly. "I feel it in my bones. They'll find Alicia Vernon."

"Well, we're not going to the police," said Dave, equally firmly.

"But Dave, we should. I'm sure A.V. is dead. And someone's just tried to kill me because we're prying too much."

"Look," said Dave. "I know that and you know that. But we don't know *who*. We can't prove anything. We won't see him again – he'll be too clever for that. We'd spend hours in a police station getting nowhere. We'd miss the rehearsal and the concert, and even if we were out in time Frank would hit the roof and send us home for sure. Let the police do their own work. I've had enough of them."

Dave was very persuasive.

"I still think we ought," said Katie doubtfully.

"*Listen* to me," said Dave. "I'm right. We'll sort it out ourselves."

Sort *what* out? Katie had a sudden terrible vision. They were together in a maze of twisting paths between high hedges. Every corner promised an exit, every turning revealed a blank dead end. Vultures circled above her; ravenous beasts padded unseen in the undergrowth. And what were they *doing* in this maze? Nothing that had happened had anything to do with them. It all concerned other, faraway people, out of their league. Until now. Becoming involved suddenly seemed a wilfully stupid act of self-laceration. For now they were *really* in it: Katie had nearly been a victim as much as Laura Merchant had been, Gerald Swordblade and Alicia Vernon probably were. She looked up at Dave.

"Dave," she said. "How can *I* have anything to do with the story in the Ballad of Little Musgrave?"

"You're getting too close to the truth," said Dave.

"But who knows that?"

"I don't know. Gwen? Sam's mum?"

Katie remembered their talk with Mrs Belling the day before. Bitterness in the voice. Pain in the eyes.

"Oh, *surely* not her!" she cried in horror. "What about Sam if her mum's involved?"

They clung to each other wordlessly for some minutes. Then Dave said, "We can't stay here all night."

"I don't want to go back yet," said Katie. "We've got hours before the theatre. Let's just go for a walk."

So they left the station and wandered arm-in-arm up Victoria Street, towards Parliament Square and Big Ben. The early evening was still warm as they pushed against the tide of commuters hurrying to Victoria station. They suddenly felt hungry, and regretted not having eaten at the station, so they slipped into a sandwich bar, then emerged and walked slowly down to the river. Here they stared across the water at the South Bank, the Festival Hall and the National Theatre, and watched river boats crowded with tourists. Surveying other, busy people made them feel insulated from the rest of the world, separated, smothered by impenetrable mystery.

"What shall we do?" said Dave at last. "We can't stand here all night."

"Let's go back," said Katie. "I feel better now. The others may cheer us up a bit."

"The Circle line from Westminster gets us there," said Dave.

"I don't think I ever want to go near a railway platform again," said Katie.

"You'll be OK," said Dave.

She was. Fifteen minutes later they emerged from the station and set off along the walkway to the heart of the Citadel Centre. As soon as they entered, they knew something was wrong. Over to the right, towards the main centre and under the four storeys of luxury flats, blue lights flashed. Police cars were parked and, even as they watched, an ambulance roared off, siren blaring, in the opposite direction. A huge knot of watching people slowly dispersed.

"What's happened?" gasped Katie.

They ran past the fountains to where it was all happening. They soon saw people they knew. Roger and Andy from the trombones were watching with an interest which struck Katie as rather ghoulish. When she asked them what had happened, Roger answered, "A bit more excitement. Some bloke fell sixty feet from the top storey."

"Ah!" said Andy. "But did he fall or was he pushed?"

"Who was he?" asked Dave.

"No idea," said Roger.

"*I* know," said a voice behind them.

They turned.

Gwen stood there, leaning against the wall separating pavement from pool as if she could not stay upright on her own.

"Who?" said Katie.

"The man I pointed out to you last night in the audience. The man who brought the message to me in Leeds. He's dead."

It was Katie's turn to lean against the wall for support.

"Yes, I've told the police," said Gwen. "They don't know who he is."

They were in a coffee bar close to the concert hall. Roger and Andy had tagged along; Katie presumed Samantha had at least temporarily ditched Roger. They listened to the afternoon's two main stories open-mouthed.

"I saw the man this afternoon at half-past five," said Gwen. "I thought he might have come out of the tube station." Katie and Dave looked at each other. "He didn't see me. He walked straight to a lift. I didn't think any more about him. But about twenty minutes later, I heard this great howl. So did everyone else; we all ran outside. We thought it was a bit of street theatre. And there he was, sprawled out on the ground. I knew him at once. Even with a green shirt and fawn trousers on instead of his sharp blue suit. When the police came, I told them all I knew. They seemed to think that because I kept seeing him, I ought to know who he was."

"Whoever he was, he tried to kill me," said Katie. She recounted the events of the afternoon.

"He might have just wanted to scare you," said Roger.

"Some scare," said Dave. "And ending up dead himself hardly an hour later? There *has* to be a pattern behind all this."

"Gwen," said Katie, "does the story in the ballad of Little Musgrave and Lady Barnard mean anything to you?"

"How do you mean?" said Gwen.

Quickly, Katie recounted what she and Dave had thought of that morning – that the story was a parallel of events of years ago; that Rosalie was Lady Barnard, Gerald was Lord Barnard, and Little Musgrave and the page were – who?

Gwen listened. As Katie spoke, she became even paler.

"Yes," she said when Katie had finished. "I know about the famous magic circle. And I know about Rosalie being killed in a fire. There were plenty to tell me even so long after it happened. But I *won't* believe Gerry had anything to do with it."

"And what about Hugo?" said Katie.

"Oh, *Hugo*," said Gwen. "I don't know what's happened to Hugo. Where is he? I don't know what more I can do to find him."

"Don't worry," said Andy. "Frank told us this morning. He's heard from him. He'll be here tomorrow."

"Why hasn't he got in touch with *me*?" cried Gwen. "That could be *anyone* who sent a message to Frank. No one's seen him since he went off last night before the concert in Hedford."

"Have you tried to contact him?" said Roger.

"How can I do more than I've done already?"

"Ring round. I keep on hearing about this Royal National Conservatoire. It's only just round the corner. Is he there? Has he gone home to Sussex? Why not try him there?"

Gwen cast him a cold look.

"I'm not quite helpless," she said. "I've tried both. He's not been to the Conservatoire and there's no answer from his home. I've no idea where Frank's supposed to have got this message from."

"Could Hugo have written the variations as a sort of coded signal?" said Dave.

"Why should he?" said Gwen. "If he suspected Rosalie was murdered, then after all this time he'd want to keep quiet about it – let sleeping dogs lie. I don't believe he'd want any harm to come to dear Laura. Or Gerry."

"What about Alicia Vernon?" said Katie.

"What do you mean?" said Gwen.

Katie told her about the newspaper report. Gwen slumped even further back into her seat.

"Oh, my God!" she said. "Hugo could have gone to Amsterdam."

"So you do think he could be involved?" said Dave.

"I don't know what to think any more," Gwen replied. "*Nothing* adds up. There's no rhyme or reason to it."

"Let's try to find some," said Dave. "What have we got?" He thought for a moment: then said, "We must write it down."

Gwen looked inside her shoulder-bag.

"My trusty Filofax," she said.

She took the pen from its loop in the spine of the diary. Then she opened the leather-bound book at a note page.

"Where do we begin?" she said.

"Anywhere," said Dave. "What about this for starters? Hugo's either involved directly in the murders or he's not."

Gwen wrote it down.

Katie said: "The murders are either done to follow a definite timetable or they're not."

Dave continued. "It's all either to do with whatever happened in the past with the magic circle, or it's not."

"So it's either a long revenge or it's not," said Katie.

"And what the revenge is for is either told in the story of Little Musgrave or it's not," said Dave.

"And if it is, Hugo either chose it deliberately as a signal to the murderer or he didn't," said Katie.

"And he dedicated the variations to particular people either because he just happens to like them or because he wants them killed," said Dave.

Gwen was writing more and more slowly. By the time she had noted down Dave's last point, she was even paler than before. She looked up from the Filofax.

"But that's an *awful* thing to say!" she gasped. "I won't believe it of my Hugo."

She put her pen down. Tears filled her eyes. Katie leant across and put her arms round her.

"You really like him, don't you?" she said.

Gwen turned a tear-stained face to her.

"I know his faults. He's conceited, arrogant and thoughtless. And perhaps he's got cause to be. But he's wonderful too. I love him. I really do. Oh, why am I telling this to you? It's because I want you to know. He wouldn't *do* this."

She dried her eyes.

"But the man who was killed this afternoon could," she said with sudden firmness.

"We don't know who he was," said Katie.

Silence again.

"There'll be a report on TV," said Andy. "Or local radio."

"Where's the nearest TV?" said Dave.

But they made no move. They sat, looking at each other.

Roger spoke.

"I know I've only just come in on this," he said. "But I think I've got most of the picture. So don't laugh if I ask an idiot question."

"Go on," said Katie.

"Well, you keep talking about some long revenge. Who's it for? Rosalie? This Ken fellow? The student Rosalie bunked off with?"

"I don't know," said Dave.

"And does it have to be a revenge at all? What about a long shutting up? What about if whoever killed Rosalie and her toyboy and whoever killed Ken – always supposing someone did and they were the same person – is saying, 'Hugo's written this piece and I think it shows I've been rumbled after all these years, so I'd better make sure all those who might suspect are silenced.'"

"That's pretty unlikely," said Andy.

"No, it's not," said Roger. "I've only just heard about

this magic circle and you said the murder victims could all be people who gave Swordblade his alibi. So the killings needn't be revenge on the ones who did the cover-up to start with. They could be done to *make sure* they stay quiet."

"That means Gerald Swordblade was the murderer," said Katie.

"But he's dead himself," said Dave.

"You don't know that," said Roger. "He's only disappeared. It could all be a big fake. He could be here, now."

"How could Gerald have killed Laura Merchant on Monday?" said Gwen. "He was visiting us in Wardminster."

"Then he's got an accomplice to share the killing with him."

"Who?" said Dave.

They were silent again. Gwen thought of a body sprawled on the paving stones under the flats by the Citadel Centre. Katie remembered a sudden push, the gleam of rails and the roar of an approaching train. Dave recalled pulling her to safety, turning and looking vainly for a green-shirted figure melting into the crowd.

"Come on," he said. "Let's find a TV or a radio."

12

But when they found a radio – in Samantha's Walkman when they located her in a bookstore on the main level – it was of no help. GLR and Capital Radio both reported the death but said that the body was unidentified.

"So he didn't even carry a driving licence or credit card," said Roger. "He didn't want to be known. Odder and odder."

"I was looking for you," said Samantha. "It's nearly time for the theatre. We don't want to upset Frank." She looked at Katie and Dave. "You two certainly don't."

Of course. The Royal Classic Theatre and *Hamlet*. In the afternoon's turmoil, Katie had forgotten.

"I'll have to get ready," she said. "I'm a mess."

"There's no time," said Samantha. "A quick spruce-up in the cloakroom's all you need."

"If only!" said Katie.

"It's seven now," said Samantha. "Frank wants us there at quarter past to give us the tickets. Let's have another coffee."

So Katie found herself at yet another table risking caffeine poisoning, while Sam was brought up to date with the theory about the ballad of Little Musgrave, their afternoon's scare and the doings of the now-dead stranger. When the account was over and her cries of "You'll have to go to the police!" were stilled, Roger spoke again.

"Katie, remember last Sunday when Hugo first introduced his variations? I said to you that F.T. was Frank. Well, I bet I'm right. Now I've heard you two, I think I know what's happened."

"Go on," said Dave.

"Right," said Roger. "Try this for size. Hugo composes his variations. He deliberately chooses *Little Musgrave* so Swordblade will know he's on to him, that he killed his own wife and her toyboy and got away with it. And Swordblade says, 'There's a lot of people who know about this because they gave me an alibi. I'll have to do them all in or they'll talk when they hear Hugo's done this piece of music.' So he waits till the variations are performed and first he gets his accomplice to kill Laura while he makes sure he's seen by us all somewhere else. Then he fakes it so everyone thinks he's dead but all the time he's nipping over to Amsterdam to kill Alicia Vernon. Then he comes back."

"Why?" said Dave. "Not to kill his accomplice?"

"Why not?" said Roger. "That's another one who knows out of the way."

"So you think Sir Gerald Swordblade is *here*, wandering round in the crowds outside?" said Katie.

"Not now," said Roger. "He'll be hiding. But he'll turn up tomorrow and he'll make sure Frank Thurlow doesn't last the evening."

"And that's his job done, is it?" said Dave.

"Oh, no," said Roger. "There's one left. Who started it all?"

"You don't mean Hugo?" said Katie.

"Of course," said Roger. "Hugo's got to go. The final confrontation. With Hugo quiet for ever, Swordblade's in the clear. Nobody's left alive to grass on him. We'll hear no more about him for a few days, then he'll turn up half dead, saying he's been stuck in a pothole for a week and what a lucky escape he's had. He'll probably say he's lost his memory as well."

"That's too easy," said Dave. "If he wants to get rid of people, why do it so publicly, drawing so much attention?"

"These artistic types," said Roger. "Show-offs, the lot of them. Besides, he wants to scare the hell out of people too."

"He seems to have succeeded with Hugo," said Katie.

Gwen stood up. The rest had almost forgotten she was still there, sitting in a corner as if she was not really with them.

"I must leave," she said. "I'm not going to *Hamlet*."

Katie saw an odd expression in her face that she didn't understand. She stood up as well.

"I *must* go to the cloakroom," she said. "I'll be back."

Outside, on the carpeted main level, surrounded by

concert- and theatre-goers, Katie spoke to Gwen.

"What Roger said upset you, didn't it?" she said. "Don't mind him. He gets mad ideas."

"He's not mad," Gwen replied. "He's *right*. I know it. Hugo's in danger. I wish I knew where he was."

"Have you no idea?"

"I've got this feeling he may be in his house in Sussex. I rang there three times today but there was no answer. I keep getting his voice on the answering machine. So I know he must be there."

"That's silly," said Katie. "It shows he's not."

"But I rang last night, after the concert. The machine was on, but there was just a noise – the tape was full. So someone's put a new one in since then. Who but Hugo? He must be there."

"It could be someone else," said Katie.

"I'm *sure* he's there," Gwen insisted.

"Then he doesn't want to be disturbed or he'd answer," said Katie.

"I don't believe that," said Gwen. "Perhaps he *can't* answer. Perhaps something's wrong. I want to know."

"How can you?"

"I want to go there and see for myself. I'm going to leave now, catch a train from Victoria and get a taxi at the other end."

Katie looked at her. Well, why shouldn't she? She'd been wanting to spend time with Hugo all this week and it wasn't her fault he'd brushed her off so effectively.

Gwen saw what was in Katie's face.

"No, it's not what you're thinking. I want to make sure he's all right. I *know* he's there."

"It's a long way to go if he's not," said Katie.

"I *know* he is," Gwen repeated stubbornly.

Katie was silent. After being so sure Alicia Vernon was dead in Amsterdam, she had no right to question other people's hunches. But she had an equally strong hunch herself. What Gwen proposed was not right.

"What if he is there?" she said. "If he's all right, he's not bothered about seeing you. If he was bothered, he'd have answered the phone. But if he's not all right—"

"That's what I mean," Gwen burst in. "He may be in danger or injured … or dead."

"Then you *can't* go," said Katie. "Tell the police."

I'm a fine one to talk, she thought.

"*I want to see for myself.*"

Katie could see her mind was made up.

"Then you shouldn't go on your own," she said.

"Who'd go with me?" said Gwen.

"I've got to get ready," said Katie.

She left Gwen while she went to the cloakroom and spruced herself up so that she felt at least respectable and refreshed. As she looked in the mirror, she thought. This was a hare-brained scheme of Gwen's but there was – from Gwen's point of view – a daft logic in it. She *shouldn't* go alone though. If she were to find Hugo dead or injured, that would be terrible for her. If she found Hugo with some girlfriend she knew nothing about, that would be nearly as bad. And what if she found neither? What if Hugo was miles away? What a waste of time and money. And what if Hugo *was* there, but there was someone else too – someone not well disposed to him or any friend who might visit? What had Roger said?

"There's only one left. Who started it all?" What if Roger was right in everything but the timetable of events and Gerald Swordblade, bent on murder, was even now approaching the house? Or there already? Or, if not Gerald, someone equally malevolent?

When Katie emerged from the cloakroom, she saw Gwen standing in the same place.

"You really shouldn't go, Gwen," she said.

"I'm going," Gwen repeated. "I'm going *now*." But she remained rooted to the spot.

"Then I'll have to tell someone," said Katie.

"Don't you *dare*!" said Gwen.

"Then I'll have to come with you myself."

Katie suddenly couldn't believe what she was saying. Hadn't she been in enough trouble that day? Still, it wouldn't matter. Gwen was bound to say she didn't want her.

"Oh, would you?" said Gwen. "That would be wonderful."

It would be fitting as well, Katie thought. They had, in a sort of way, been in this together from the start. She wouldn't easily forget their talk in the small hours under the cypress tree at Pegham Priory.

"But you mustn't," Gwen continued. "You've been in danger yourself today. You deserve a quiet evening in the theatre."

Well, it was a lovely thought. But Katie knew she'd hate every minute, thinking of Gwen going alone into the dark...

By the box office, the theatre party was gathering. Frank was checking names and giving out tickets. Katie made her mind up.

"Stay here," she said. "Give me fifteen minutes. If I'm not with you by then, go without me. I've got to try and slip out so no one notices."

Gwen nodded. She was obviously pleased.

"I'll pay for the fares," she said. "Fifteen minutes then."

Katie joined the others. She wondered whether she should tell Dave. No, not yet. A plan of campaign was forming in her mind. She pushed her way to the front to where Liz was giving out tickets.

"Can I have a gangway seat?" she said.

"With pleasure," said Liz. "Most people are clamouring for the middle."

Katie took two: one for Dave next to her. They filed into the theatre. She noticed that, unlike most other theatres she had been in, entrance to the auditorium was made at the end of each row. So, as long as she timed it right before the doors were closed, she should be able to slip out unnoticed.

She bought a programme and felt in the pocket of her jeans for a ballpoint pen, then she and Dave took their seats, Katie at the end of the row. She opened her programme and took out the pen.

The theatre was full. The house lights dimmed. She scribbled furiously on her programme – *Am going to Hugo's place in Sussex with Gwen. It's important. Cover for me.*

Then, hoping he wouldn't read it till the lights went up at the interval, she shoved the programme, open at her message, into Dave's hands, whispered "I must go to

125

the loo again," in his ear, kissed him on the cheek and was gone before he turned round.

The foyer was almost empty but Gwen was no longer alone. A large, even formidable, woman stood with her, wearing a white top and a long, light-blue skirt. Both the face and the clothes struck definite but quite separate chords in Katie's memory.

"Katie," said Gwen. "I'd like you to meet Fiona Tankerton."

The opera singer. One of the magic circle. Another F.T.

"Fiona *lives* here," said Gwen. "She has a flat right next to the Centre. I never knew that."

"I've known Gwen ever since her Conservatoire days," said Fiona, extending her hand to Katie. "I thought I just *had* to be here tomorrow to listen to Hugo's new work. But I see I'm too late to meet dear Frank again tonight, unless I wait until *Hamlet*'s over. Let's us three go and have a drink and you can tell me all about yourselves."

Katie looked at Gwen. Had she changed her mind? Surely the escape from *Hamlet* hadn't been for nothing?

"Sorry, Fiona," said Gwen. "Katie and I are on an errand. We've got a train to catch."

She turned to go. But now Katie delayed. Something had occurred to her.

"Miss Tankerton," she said. "If you live in the flats, you must know about the man who was killed this afternoon."

"Terrible, wasn't it?" said Fiona. "No, I wasn't in at the time. But I've heard all about it since. He fell over the wall just outside my own flat. Nobody knows if it was an accident, suicide, or if someone pushed him. I've seen the police and told them what little I can. Poor man. Nobody seems to know who he was. Ah well, I mustn't keep you if you're in a hurry."

They left her and walked quickly outside and towards the underground station.

It wasn't until she was sitting on yet another Circle line train going towards Victoria that Katie shook her head as if to clear it and thought: Why am I doing this? Has this afternoon's experience sent me completely round the twist? For this, she was certain, was a complete wild goose chase. It was just as well Gwen was paying.

And now came another thought. What if Hugo was there – and really pleased to see Gwen turn up? What about her? She'd just be a big gooseberry. What total embarrassment. And what if Gwen's hunch was wrong, Hugo wasn't at home and the house was dark, locked and impregnable? Where would she sleep that night? She didn't fancy eight hours in a ditch. Why hadn't she thought of that?

The train reached Victoria. For the second time that day she found herself on the Brighton side of Victoria station. But now it was not jostlingly crowded and Gwen hardly had to queue for the two single tickets to Three Bridges.

While she waited, Katie saw a placard outside a news stand:

DEATH FALL MAN NAMED

Gwen joined her with the tickets. Katie was unwilling

127

to buy her second evening paper of the day, but Gwen needed no prompting. She picked up a paper at once and they found what they wanted under *Latest news*.

> *Police this evening named the man who fell to death this afternoon at the Citadel Centre as Ronald Stubbs (35) of Birmingham. Mr Stubbs was identified as a known criminal who had just completed a six-year sentence for armed robbery and grievous bodily harm.*

Gwen shuddered. "I *knew* he was evil," she said.

A cold feeling swept through Katie's stomach. Yes, he *would* have pushed her on to the rails without compunction. Even so...

"It's peculiar," she said. "He's not exactly the sort you'd expect to be going to concerts to hear you playing the piano."

Gwen shuddered again. "*Don't,*" she said.

The train was nearly empty. It left on time and deposited them at Three Bridges station on time as well. They walked away from the echoing platforms to the taxi rank. Two minutes later they were sitting in the back of a Nissan Primera, heading away from Crawley into the Sussex countryside.

Outside, everything seemed very dark. Katie might have been scared half out of her wits that afternoon – but at least it was in light, noise and surrounded by people. These tracts of deserted woods and surrounding fields were oppressive to her.

They were going through a village. Gwen peered forward.

"Take the next left," she said, then: "Here will do."

The taxi stopped. They got out and Gwen handed over what seemed to Katie a vast amount of money. The taxi reversed in the road and was gone, its red tail light dwindling away in the dusk. Katie suddenly felt very lonely, standing on the grass verge of a dark road miles from anywhere she knew.

Gwen walked through open gates up a drive with a two-storeyed detached house at the end. Katie could see no lights.

"This is where Hugo lives," said Gwen.

Katie didn't answer. She was thinking of her empty seat at the Citadel Theatre: of Dave distracted, Frank and Liz furious.

And she thought of *Hamlet*. She knew the play from A-level. She looked at her watch. At about this moment, Hamlet should be stabbing with his rapier through the arras in his mother's room, shouting "How now! A rat?" and realizing what he had done when he found the dead body of Polonius.

13

As she slipped out of the theatre, Katie didn't hear Dave whisper, "But you've only just been. Is something wrong with your bladder?"

Stage lights came up. *She'll have to be quick*, Dave thought.

At Elsinore Castle, Bernardo took over from Francisco on sentry duty. Dave looked worriedly round. The doors at the end of each row were closed; nobody would be allowed back in.

At first, he felt a mixture of disappointment and amusement. Soon it changed to annoyance. *That was really stupid*, he thought.

On stage, Hamlet was listening to the message brought by his father's ghost. But Dave's interest in the play had gone. All he could do was keep repeating the question, *Why has she done this?* Suddenly, words spoken by Hamlet chimed in exactly with his thoughts.

"*Oh, my prophetic soul.*"

Immediately the suspicion he was forming presented itself as fact. *She'd deliberately gone off somewhere without him.*

He nearly got up at once to tear open the door at the end of the row and dash out. *No, what's the point? Stay where you are. Keep calm until the interval.*

The interval, though, seemed a long time coming. For a play he had always been told was fast-moving, this production went at the speed of paint drying. But at last Hamlet strode off with the resolve:

> "...*The play's the thing*
> *Wherein I'll catch the conscience of the king.*"

The stage lights dimmed, the house lights came up. Dave found the programme on his knees, open at the page Katie had scrawled on.

Am going to Hugo's place in Sussex with Gwen. It's important. Cover for me.

He looked at it uncomprehendingly. Everybody in the row had stood up to go out. Next to him, Roger was shaking him by the shoulder and saying, "Come on, Dave. Shift yourself."

Dave rose dazedly and shuffled out. *I have to tell someone. This is too much for me on top of everything today. Roger's the one. He's a mate – and he's thought a lot about this whole affair.*

Once out of the auditorium, he spoke to Roger.

"What do you make of this?" he said, showing him the programme.

Roger looked at the message, looked at Dave, seemed to sum things up at once and said, "You've got problems."

"We all have," said Dave. "What can we do?"

"Well, we're not telling Frank for a start," said Roger. "We'll sort this out ourselves."

"How?"

"Where in Sussex?" said Roger.

"Not a clue."

"Wait here."

Ginny Belling was close by, talking to Arthur Armitage and Liz about the play. Roger quietly joined the conversation.

"It's a lovely production," Samantha's mum was saying.

"Bit slow," replied Arthur. "Some operas move quicker."

"*Hamlet* would make a good opera," Roger said, as if he'd been with them all the time. "Hugo should write it."

"Someone's already tried," said Arthur. "A man called Thomas in the nineteenth century. Not much good, though. Not like Verdi's Shakespeare operas."

"Well, Hugo could do it," said Roger. "A really good modern version. Pity he's back in Sussex now and not here watching it."

"Who says he's in Sussex?" said Liz.

"Isn't he? I thought he always went there, to ... what's the name of the place?"

"How should I know?" said Arthur.

"Oh, Gwen told me," said Ginny Belling. "He's got this beautiful house – what's it called now? I know – Rowan Lodge. It's at the edge of a village a few miles from Crawley. Lower Lambsfield. That's it. Sounds lovely. What do *you* think of the play so far, Roger?"

"Why so interested, Roger?" said Liz.

But Roger didn't answer. He was back with Dave.

"Right," he said. "We've got to think fast. I've a feeling your Katie's done something very silly indeed."

Katie followed Gwen to the front door. Their feet scrunched on gravel. They skirted a lawn. A double garage stood by the side of the house, its doors firmly closed.

Gwen rang the doorbell. Chimes pealed through the house.

Nobody answered.

"I knew it," said Katie. "It's been a waste of time."

"I *know* he's here," replied Gwen.

She uselessly tried the door handle, then walked to the double garage, produced a tiny torch from her shoulder bag and shone it through the window.

"See?" she said. "The Porsche is inside."

Katie looked as well. Its sleek lines were unmistakable.

"He's in the house," said Gwen. "And he's in trouble."

She stood for a moment, thinking.

"There's something else wrong," she said. "What is it?"

She stood looking at the unlit bulk of the house as darkness finally fell.

"Got it," she said. "Hugo had security lights fitted. We should have been bathed in light as soon as we came up the drive. And if the security lights aren't on, then the burglar alarm isn't either. Why not?"

Gwen was more resourceful than Katie had given her credit for.

"Come on," she said. "We'll explore all round the outside."

"What's the point?" said Katie.

"If the burglar alarm's not working, it's either switched off or been broken. Someone might have got in already. We might get in the same way."

Suddenly, Katie didn't like what was happening. She wasn't sure about this new commanding and quick-thinking Gwen. She remembered the afternoon's scare. Was she being led into another trap?

"If the house has been broken into, the intruder might still be there," she said.

"I doubt it," Gwen replied. "It's worth the risk."

She was walking round the house, examining the windows. All seemed intact and firmly closed. At the rear, facing a patio and a long lawn, were sliding glass doors. Cautiously, Gwen tried the handle of one. The door slid smoothly open.

"I told you," she said and slipped inside.

Suddenly, Gwen seemed menacing – a featureless figure in the dark. The patio door was a gateway to doom.

"Come on in. What are you waiting for?" she hissed.

Unwillingly, Katie followed. They stood in a large room. Katie could just make out the shape of a grand piano. Gwen shone the torch round: booklined shelves, pictures hanging on white walls.

"Aren't you going to switch the light on?" Katie said.

Let whoever's waiting here for me get it over with, she thought.

"Not yet," said Gwen. "Listen."

Night noises crept faintly into the room. Far away in the village, cars started and people shouted. The pubs were closing.

Suddenly, Katie's fears evaporated.

"Gwen," she said. "It's no good. The house is empty."

"Put the light on now," said Gwen.

Katie did so. In the brightness, they both gasped.

The room had obviously been searched. Not ransacked by a burglar frustrated at finding nothing worth taking, but certainly combed through with care. The drawers of a big desk had been taken out and a filing cabinet opened. Papers and files littered the place. Doors of display cabinets swung open.

"Is anything gone?" said Katie.

"I've no idea," said Gwen. "His word processor and hi-fi are still here. Hugo's got some valuable musical instruments. We'd better have a look for them."

They went from room to room. Nothing seemed to have been touched. The kitchen was neat and tidy, though Gwen could not say if the traditional and weird-looking instruments hanging from the walls or placed on tables were all present and correct.

"Hugo could have been looking for something himself," said Katie.

"Then he was interrupted," said Gwen.

They completed their search, leaving every light on. Then they sat together on the stairs.

"What do we do?" said Gwen.

Her new-found leadership powers seemed to evaporate. Looking at her, Katie wondered how she could have thought her a threat.

"Let's go to the police," said Katie. "We'll tell them there's been a break-in."

"They'll say we did it," said Gwen.

"How can they?"

And then all the lights went out.

The sudden darkness was shocking. Gwen screamed.

"Sssshh!" hissed Katie.

They listened. From downstairs came a faint rumble and then a click. Gwen found her torch. They fumbled their way slowly by its light back to the patio doors through which they had entered.

They were locked.

"We're trapped," said Gwen.

I was right after all, Katie thought. *What possessed me to come here?*

"The point is," said Roger urgently, "do you want to watch the rest of the play or stay out and *do* something?"

"What *can* we do?" said Dave.

"Now we know where they are, we can go there ourselves."

"Don't be daft. After this afternoon I'm about broke."

"Don't worry about that," said Roger.

"Anyway, why should you get yourself in bother with Frank?"

"Don't worry about that either. Do we go back in or not?"

People were re-entering the theatre. Dave suddenly realized there was no way he could join them.

"All right, what do we do?" he said.

* * *

They really were trapped. Every window had a security lock and small panes of glass, so even if they smashed one they couldn't crawl out. Every door had a high-security lock.

Gwen flopped into an armchair.

"I'm sorry, Katie," she said. "What a mess I've made."

"We'll telephone for help," said Katie.

She had noticed a telephone on the desk. She felt around for it and lifted the receiver. Then she put it down again.

"Dead," she said. "We're cut off."

They said nothing for several seconds. Then Gwen stood up, stumbled across littered files and papers to the patio door, looked through it and shouted at the top of her voice, "Help! Let us out! Let us out!"

"That's no good," said Katie.

"How about this?" said Roger. "My folks are away. 'If you can go on tour, then so can we,' they said."

"So?" said Dave.

"Well, you know where I live. We can get a direct Thameslink train from the tube station here, no trouble."

"What for?" said Dave.

"So we can pick up my mum's old Metro," said Roger. "I've passed my test and I know where the keys are. We'll *drive* down."

"Brilliant!" said Dave.

But shouting through the patio door did have an effect. There was movement. An indistinct figure almost darker than the darkness appeared at the door. There was another click and rumble. The door opened and night air flooded in again.

Gwen and Katie clung together as the figure stood in the open doorway and faced them.

"Gwen?" it said questioningly.

"*Hugo!*" gasped Gwen.

Hugo it was. He looked wild, dishevelled, dazed.

"Oh, Hugo, you're all right," said Gwen. She stumbled forward and fell into his outstretched arms.

"What in God's name are you doing here?" he said.

Gwen sobbed with relief. Katie wished she was a long way away.

"Wait a minute," said Hugo. "I have to switch the mains on."

He extricated himself from Gwen's clutches and disappeared into the hallway. A moment later, the lights went up and Hugo reappeared. Now they saw there was a bruise on the side of his face and blood on his shirt.

"How many more shocks am I due for today?" he said.

The Thameslink train whisked them northwards and a brisk ten-minute walk through quiet streets brought them to Roger's house. He produced a key and let himself in the front door. Dave watched as Roger went to a kitchen drawer and produced the car keys.

"No worries," he said.

He wrote on the kitchen notice board: *Thursday night. Borrowed Metro. R.*

"They might come back early," he said. "I don't want them reporting a theft."

They went outside. Roger opened the garage and two

minutes later the Metro, still cold, was leaping unevenly down the road.

Hugo pointed to his livid bruise.

"I thought I was trapping the person who did this," he said. "I got a shock when I heard your voice shouting."

But he seemed rather touched that they had come all that way because they were worried about him.

"Have I got news for you? A lot's happened, some not nice."

"Tell us," said Gwen.

"Where to start?" said Hugo. "I've had some real shocks today. I've had a visitation from the past, I've heard things that are so incredible I can't quite take them in. I've been burgled, hit on the head, tied up, dumped in the woods, got myself free, broken back in to my own house. Oh, I could a tale unfold…"

"You've been hit. You're bleeding," said Gwen. "Let's get you into the kitchen and see to you."

Within a minute, Hugo was sitting on a kitchen chair and Gwen had found a first-aid box. She was bathing the bruise and washing a nasty graze while Katie looked for antiseptic and plasters.

"First things first," said Gwen. "How did you get this?"

"I had every intention of going to London this morning," said Hugo. "I had a visitor last night; he stayed over and left mid-morning. Then I went out to unlock the garage. I was jumped on from behind and hit over the head – out like a light. Woke up later – I'd been dumped in the woods behind the house. Tied up, plaster over my mouth – I couldn't believe what had happened. I suppose whoever did it thought I'd be found by someone walking in the woods. Well, today no one was. I've spent all this time trying to get free. Don't believe what they say in books. Rubbing your way through rope on a tree branch is not easy. When I got free I watched to see if anyone was still in the house. I'd just decided it was safe to go back when I saw two shadows flitting round the place and then all the lights going on. I keep a spare patio door key safe in a shed in case I shut myself out – I did once. I thought I'd lock the intruders in, switch the electricity off at the mains and get the police. Then I heard you shouting and got another big shock."

"But *who* hit you?" said Gwen.

"No idea," said Hugo. "I'd better start again at the real beginning. You know I was upset yesterday, after that police interview. I meant what I said then. I'd like to cut the hand off that wrote the notes of these blasted variations. I could only think of one thing: A.V. in Carteret Woods. I was convinced Alicia was going to be murdered, like Laura and probably Gerald. And it would all be my fault. I drove down to her house. But the police picked me up and told me she wasn't even there. I felt a real fool. But thankful."

Gwen and Katie looked at each other. Gwen opened her mouth to interrupt but Katie soundlessly mouthed "Not yet" at her.

"Anyway, when the police let me go, I thought I'd come here, have a good night's sleep and, like I said, drive up to London this morning. But no sooner had I got in the house than the phone rang. And guess who it was."

"No idea," said Gwen.

"Bill Weston. A real blast from the past. I hadn't seen him for – well, it must be ten years or more."

Bill Weston? The name rang a tiny bell in Katie's mind.

"Didn't he once run the conducting course?" said Gwen.

"The very same."

Of course. Sam's mum had mentioned him. One of the magic circle, but who never really made it.

"It was amazing," said Hugo. "He told me he was staying in the village, remembered I lived here, asked if he could come round next morning for a chat and a drink for old times' sake. 'Don't wait till tomorrow, Bill,' I said. 'Come round now.'"

"And then what?" said Gwen.

"He turned up in a taxi half an hour later. Of course, he was full of Laura's murder and Gerry's disappearance. So I started talking about the variations."

"What about the variations?" said Gwen.

"Well, I wrote them for a reason. Didn't you know?"

Gwen looked at him but said nothing.

"It's because the ballad story is the same as what happened years ago, isn't it?" said Katie.

Hugo seemed to notice Katie almost for the first time.

"How do you know that?" he said.

"Dave and me, we worked it out after what Mrs Belling told us," said Katie. "We decided Rosalie Swordblade was Lady Barnard, and Sir Gerald was Lord Barnard. Little Musgrave was the student Rosalie went off with."

"Julian," said Hugo. "Julian Stubbs."

Stubbs? Where had she heard that name recently?

"Go on," said Hugo. "You're doing well so far."

"But we don't know who the page was," said Katie. "If it was Ken Vanstone, he should have been rewarded for being right, not murdered for being wrong. We thought the page might be you."

"No way," said Hugo.

"And the murder victims were all people who had given the murderer an alibi the night the cottage burnt down – in case, once it was in the open again because of the variations, they'd talk."

"Far-fetched but clever," said Hugo. "So you think the murderer of Laura and the murderer, if there was one, of Rosalie and Julian and the murderer – if he wasn't just a random mugger – of Ken are all one and the same person. Who's that?"

"Sir Gerald Swordblade. He disappeared on Tuesday to make us think he's been murdered as well. He'll turn up again when it's all over," said Katie.

"But he was with us on Monday."

"He's got an accomplice. We know who it is."

"Was," corrected Gwen.

Hugo was quiet for a moment. Then he said, "Now for my biggest surprise on a day full of them. I always thought that if anyone killed Rosalie and Julian, it had to be Gerry. But today I found out it wasn't. So you'll have to think again. And so will I – about a lot of things I'd taken for granted for years."

14

Roger eased the Metro on to the motorway. He and Dave had hardly exchanged a word since leaving the house. But now Dave spoke.

"What are we going to do when we get there?"

"Rescue them from a fate worse than death," Roger replied. "I told you: Hugo's in trouble. Someone's after him. Whoever it is won't let two moonstruck girls stand in his way."

"You sexist pig," said Dave.

"Bred in the bone," said Roger. "I feel like St George."

"And I feel like Stan Laurel," said Dave.

Now they had reached a point of no return, he was feeling that this sudden exodus was rather daft.

"But weren't you one of the people who gave Gerald Swordblade an alibi?" said Katie.

"What makes you think that?" said Hugo.

"Sam's mum said you were in this famous magic circle."

"So?"

"They all swore they were with Gerald Swordblade that night."

"I suppose they did, those who could. Not me, though. I wasn't there. I was in hospital with appendicitis. Except for what I read in the papers and was told, I knew nothing."

"But Sam's mum said—"

"Well, why shouldn't she? I *was* one of this inner circle. But I wasn't there to give an alibi. And I'm not sure I would have done if I'd had to, except that…"

"What?" said Gwen.

"You've got to remember, Gerry was like a god to us. He *made* some of us. Nobody wanted to believe he'd done wrong, so keeping quiet would be easy. Besides, any pitch sticking to Gerry would tar them as well. That's what I always thought."

"What changed your mind?" said Katie.

"It's what Bill said this morning. All my life I've had this tearing suspicion that Gerry torched his own house with his wife and Julian inside it, and that all my friends had clammed up. And now, after all these years, along comes Bill, who was there, and tells me it wasn't like that at all. They weren't clamming up for Gerry. The person they were covering up for was Fiona."

"Fiona Tankerton who we saw this evening?" gasped Katie.

"I don't believe it," said Gwen.

"Bill made it sound very plausible. Gerry didn't need

144

to have an alibi that night, he said. Everybody knew where Gerry was. It was Fiona who went missing, along with Ken. I knew that Julian had more interests in life than his violin – he had more girlfriends than you've had hot dinners. And I knew there were mutterings about him and both Fiona and Rosalie. I also know Fiona's a strong-minded woman who doesn't like being crossed. But what Bill said would never have occurred to me in a million years."

"Which was?"

"Fiona killed them. Ken Vanstone told her Rosalie had gone off with Julian. Fiona terrorized him into going with her to the cottage and made him help her do the business."

"So the magic circle covered up for Fiona because they thought she'd done it?" said Gwen.

"I don't think they wanted to think about it," said Hugo. "They all vouched for Fiona just to stick together, not to save her from being a double murder suspect. Anyway, the police never came up with anything but an accidental fire with the victims overcome by fumes. But I think that after Ken was murdered some wondered. Bill says Laura did. So did Alicia. So did he."

"Did Gerry?"

"Never. No more did I," said Hugo. "But Bill said he had thought it all along. He was convinced after Ken was murdered."

"By Fiona, to shut him up, you mean?" said Katie.

"It looks like it. Ken was turning into a nervous wreck – I remember that. I was really worried about him. So was Frank."

"So why didn't he go to the police about it?" said Katie.

"There was a secret meeting of the inner circle after Rosalie and Julian died. All sorts of rumours were flying round. A lot of people didn't like our inner circle. They thought we were elitist, too big for our boots, next in line to God. And that's right: it's what we thought. I feel ashamed of it now. But the circle met and decided that whatever they thought, whatever they suspected about each other. they'd keep up a united front. They swore an oath, a bond they said they'd never break. Bill says Fiona made them do it. There were Fiona, Laura, Gerry, Bill himself, Ken and Alicia at this meeting. They went in shouting at each other and they came out tight-lipped, vowing silence for ever."

Gwen said at once: "But poor Ken had such a weight on his conscience that he couldn't keep quiet."

"And paid the price," said Katie.

"That's about it," said Hugo.

"Then Fiona's a monster," said Gwen.

"Yes," said Hugo. "The famous Fiona, darling of the opera world. She was a serial killer."

"But who's doing the murders now, then?" said Katie.

"Well, like you said, someone's shutting everybody up. But it isn't Gerry. If Bill's right, it's Fiona."

There was a long silence as this sank in.

"So much for the nice lady in blue I met outside the theatre," said Katie. "And Dave and I were wrong about the ballad of Little Musgrave."

"So was I," said Hugo.

"So why *did* you write it?" said Gwen.

"'A word to the wise.' 'If the cap fits, wear it.' 'He that hath ears to hear, let him hear,'" said Hugo.

"What?" said Gwen.

"Two people I knew died. My best friend was murdered. All my life I've been racked with suspicion about it. Nobody ever told me. Not even Alicia. That was half the reason we split up: I *knew* she was keeping something back from me. That damned oath they took. Well, I've always been interested in folk music. I don't know when it was that I realized Little Musgrave told the same story I believed had happened with Gerry, Julian and Rosalie. But as the years went on I got more and more the idea that if I wrote music based on that ballad I'd be sending a message – 'To whom it may concern, *this* is what I think happened. You five – Bill, Laura, Gerry, Alicia, Fiona – are the ones who could tell me whether I'm right or not.' I didn't necessarily want an answer. I just wanted to tell them I knew."

"But you didn't know after all," said Gwen.

"So it would appear," said Hugo.

"You said five names then," said Katie. "Why not five variations? Why not one for Bill?"

"Because I never rated him," Hugo replied. "I got on well with him, though Alicia couldn't stand him. He just had no talent. But Gerry thought he had – so in with the rest of us he came."

"I see," said Katie. "And is F.T. Fiona Tankerton or Frank Thurlow?"

"Funny, that," said Hugo. "In a sort of way it could be both. Fiona was at the heart of things, Frank wasn't. Ken, Frank and I were friends. Ken's murder hit Frank hard, like it did me. We could never bring ourselves to talk about it at the Conservatoire. I lost track of Frank afterwards. But when he turned up last year with your commission, I thought: Right, Frank, you can be in this as well. I'll make you look back and tell me what you think. The funny thing is, I don't believe any of this has so much as crossed Frank's mind."

"Did anyone besides Frank know?" said Gwen.

Katie was thinking.

"Fiona must have if she's behind all the new murders," she said. "You don't think up such a scheme on the spur of the moment."

"Well, I spread it around the Conservatoire," said Hugo. "And she's often there. I didn't tell Gerry directly, but I made sure enough people knew so it would filter through to him. Anyone could find out when the performances were."

"But just a minute," said Gwen. "What about the message I brought you from the man in Leeds? About Ken getting in touch with you now you've given him the key?"

"That gave me the shock of my life," Hugo replied. "Ken's dead. Someone knew what I was doing and was planning a very dirty game. I thought it could only be one person – Gerry. I was looking forward to this week – a bit of peace for a change. But I couldn't have it. I had to get down and sort things out with Gerry straight away. I went to his flat at the Conservatoire. I meant to have a flaming row with him. But he obviously hadn't got a clue what I was talking about. He must have thought I was off my trolley. I went back to the Priory that night, but I couldn't settle. I had to be off again, back to London, spending all day trying to get in touch with people to get some idea of who it might have been. I rang Laura and we spoke, but she knew nothing. I tried to get hold of Fiona, but she wasn't around. I rang Alicia and kept getting her answering machine. I was so surprised to see Gerry on Monday at Wardminster. He apologized to me. I wasn't very gracious but we were on good terms again. I'm glad of that now. So I thought everything was fine: my suspicions meant nothing and I could just enjoy my music for its own sake. And then Laura was murdered. What was I supposed to think? I *knew* it was no coincidence. But who could I tell? On Tuesday, I had to get away. I drove into the country, parked the car and walked for miles. On Wednesday I heard about Gerry. By now, all I could think about was seeing Alicia. I'd decided before the police saw me in Hedford. I told Frank where I was going and went down to Alicia's straight away. But she wasn't there. Mercifully, this time the sequence didn't work."

Gwen looked at Katie. Katie nodded. Gwen spoke.

"So you've not heard the news."

"I've had no chance," said Hugo.

"Alicia was with the PPO in Amsterdam. She's gone missing. The police are looking for her."

Under the bruise, Hugo turned pale.

"Don't speak," said Gwen. "Just think."

"It's a nightmare," Hugo eventually said. "What if Gerry and Alicia are dead? Who is it who can go round Europe killing people at will? Fiona? Is it likely? Three dead?"

"Four," said Gwen.

"How so?"

They told him of the man Katie stalked to the Science Museum.

"It would have been five if he'd pushed me off the platform," said Katie.

Hugo said nothing. He passed his hand wearily over his eyes. A thought occurred to Katie.

"Hugo, what was the name of the student killed with Rosalie?"

"Julian. Julian Stubbs."

She recalled the paper they had read at Victoria. Ronald Stubbs.

"The same name as a dead criminal," she said.

"Is that coincidence too?" said Gwen.

Despite bruise and dressing, Hugo pounded his head.

"Lost in a maze," he said. "What possessed me to write that cursed music?"

Roger and Dave were arguing. They had come off the end of the M23 and were trying to cope with roads they had never seen before. Now they were in a layby, peering at a road map.

"I told you to turn right three miles back for Lower Lambsfield," Dave said irritably.

"Yes, when I was passing the turn. It was too late then. I've been looking for another turning."

"Just reverse and we'll go back," said Dave.

Muttering to himself, Roger did so. The Metro chugged back the way they had come.

* * *

"Hugo," said Katie. "Your house has been burgled. Hadn't you better check if anything's missing?"

Hugo stood up. "I feel OK now," he said. "Let's look."

As he went through his desk and filing cabinet, put things back in order and tidied up, he talked.

"Whoever's doing this knows everything: knows what's happening on our tour, knows where all the victims are and where they're going."

"Could it be Fiona?" said Gwen.

"Why not? She knows everybody in the musical world. She can find out anything she wants."

"And you think she'd really do all this just to keep an ancient alibi intact?" said Katie. "It seems more likely to draw attention to her."

"Perhaps she wants to," said Hugo. "Gerry said on Monday that she was retiring. 'While I'm still at the top,' she'd told him. Well, what better way to go for someone as dramatic as Fiona?"

"But where does Stubbs fit in?"

"No idea. Perhaps he helped Fiona."

"Not if he was related to the man she killed," said Gwen.

"And what's going to happen to F.T. tomorrow?" said Katie.

Hugo changed the subject.

"That's it," he said. "There's only one set of things missing. All my notes and manuscripts for the variations."

"Here's the turning," said Dave. "Left here."

"I know," said Roger, signalling. "*Stupid clown!*"

He slammed the brakes on and the Metro slewed across the road. The tail-lights of the car that had turned right across them disappeared down the road they were about to take.

"That idiot nearly killed us," Dave shouted. "These BMW drivers think they own the road."

"Did you get his number?" said Roger.

"No, but the car was white," said Dave.

"I've a good mind to chase him and tell him what I think," said Roger.

"What, a humble Metro chasing a Bimmer?" said Dave.

"Well, it looks like he's going our way," said Roger."

"My burglar took what I was going to burn anyway," said Hugo.

"Why?" said Gwen.

"For the same reason," said Katie. "A ritual cleansing."

"That's very perceptive," said Hugo.

"This gets weirder," said Gwen. "Aren't you afraid your burglar will come back? Especially since he's broken your alarm and security lights."

Roger drove along the main street of Lower Lambsfield.

"Hadn't we better stop and ask the way?" said Dave.

"Not yet," said Roger. "There's the Bimmer. I'm following it."

"We haven't got *time* for that," said Dave.

"You're right, I suppose," said Roger unwillingly.

The BMW was now ahead of them, being driven with

great care. At the end of the street it turned right. Three men, obviously lately out of the pub, were swaying along the pavement.

"They'll have to do," said Roger.

He stopped, wound the window down and asked the way to Rowan Lodge. Giving it took the trio a full two minutes. In the end, Roger and Dave took the same turning as the BMW.

"I'll get him after all," said Roger.

They passed down a narrow road through dark woods. Set back from the road and surrounded by trees were large, imposing houses.

"If the Bimmer man lives in one of these," said Dave, "I'm not knocking on his front door and calling him outside."

"He nearly killed us," said Roger grimly.

"Rowan Lodge is the fourth on the left," said Dave.

"Got it," said Roger.

He was just about to signal left and turn into the drive when he let out a shout.

"There's the Bimmer!"

The white car was parked half on, half off the grass verge, about ten metres to the other side of the entrance.

"I'm going to have a look," said Roger.

"Oh, forget him," said Dave irritably. "There's no one in it. You can't go on holding grudges against mad drivers all your life – you'd never get two miles without a punch-up."

So Roger turned up the drive after all.

"There's someone there," said Dave.

In the headlights' glare they saw a man. He was

creeping round the side of the house with his back to them. He carried a square object in one hand, an unidentifiable bundle in the other.

"He's not friendly," Dave whispered.

"Hugo?" Roger called.

The man straightened and turned. He was tall, thin, dressed in sweatshirt, jeans and trainers.

"That's a petrol can he's got," said Roger.

"He's not Hugo," said Dave.

The man didn't hesitate. The instant he saw them, he ran straight for and then past them, swinging the can wildly and barging them both aside. Dave made a despairing lunge, but only managed to grab uselessly at the bundle.

The man was gone, through the entrance and down the road. They picked themselves up and raced after him, just in time to see the BMW's tail-lights disappearing down the road.

They stopped and breathlessly turned back to the house.

"I knew the Bimmer man was up to no good," said Roger. "That was petrol in his can. I smelt it and heard it sloshing."

"The bundle was soft," said Dave. "Like cloth."

"Oily rags?" said Roger.

"Surely he wasn't going to burn the place down?" said Dave.

The front door opened. Hugo stood framed in the light.

"Who's there?" he called.

"You're lucky it's only us," replied Roger.

15

Five people sat drinking coffee in Hugo's kitchen. "I was reconnecting the burglar alarm and lights when I heard the noise outside," said Hugo. "You say you disturbed someone trying to get in the house?"

"No," said Roger. "Not just trying to get in. He looked like he was trying to burn it down."

"That rings a bell for you, doesn't it?" said Dave.

"Tall, not young, drives a white BMW," said Roger.

"I can't believe this," said Hugo. "Did you get the BMW's number?"

Dave and Roger looked at each other.

"You twerp," said Dave.

"I thought you did," said Roger.

"I don't think it was a letter to show the year," said Dave. "It was a personal plate, the sort that nearly spells a word."

"Help me finish reconnecting the alarm and lights,"

said Hugo. "Then we'll recap on everything we know."

It was done. The day's intruder had merely pulled wires out, and a few minutes' work with the screwdriver put all to rights. The telephone was a different matter; the cable was cut outside. A call to BT could wait until morning.

Then they talked for hours, going over everything that had happened, trying to find a pattern.

"It's a maze," said Hugo. "Nothing adds up. If Bill's right about Fiona, *why* is she doing it? Why was the man Stubbs killed this afternoon? Was he related to Julian?"

"And is Gerry dead?" said Gwen.

"Is Alicia?" said Katie. "Was Bill Weston's visit here last night just coincidence?"

"Who was it who carved us up in the BMW and ran away?" said Roger.

"Who was it dressed in light blue that Stubbs went to see in the museum? And why did Stubbs *definitely* try to kill Katie on Victoria tube station?" said Dave.

"I don't like saying this," said Roger. "But if someone tried to kill Katie this afternoon, you don't think tonight's effort that we interrupted was him trying to finish the job off properly?"

There was silence.

"Impossible," said Gwen. "Who would know she was here?"

"I get the feeling," said Katie, "of someone at the centre of all this. Like a spider in the middle of a web. Knowing everything, seeing everything. Making everything in the plan go like clockwork, to a timetable."

"Until today," said Dave.

"And who ruined it all?" said Gwen.

"Katie did," said Roger. "She was the one asking questions, seeing patterns, getting in the way. Someone sees this. So friend Stubbs accidentally on purpose tries to heave her over the platform edge. And the long streak in the Bimmer tries to finish it off."

"I don't want to believe that," said Katie.

"Well, there's one thing," said Gwen. "If someone actually came round to burn the house down, at least Hugo's Musgrave manuscript wouldn't have perished in the flames."

"Was the day's intruder the same as the night's?" said Dave.

"How many people have been to this house today with malice in their hearts?" said Hugo. "Two? Three?"

"Or just one?" said Katie.

Hugo didn't answer.

Two o'clock came before they slept. Dave and Roger crashed out on armchairs. Hugo offered Katie a bed in a spare room, which she gratefully took. Then he and Gwen disappeared together. Ask no questions, Katie thought. By eight next morning, Hugo was putting together a breakfast of sorts and assuring them that, if their absence had been noted, he would see it all right with Frank.

Afterwards, they went to the garage where the Porsche waited.

"You'd think a self-respecting thief would have taken that," said Roger.

Nothing had been touched. Hugo started it first time.

Gwen got into the Porsche. Hugo looked out of the window.

"Don't worry about Frank," he said. "We'll be there before you. I'll have made things all right before you arrive."

The Porsche was gone, with a scrunch on the gravel and a sharp bite from the exhaust. Roger watched it.

"Great," he said. "You notice none of us were offered a lift in it."

"Why should we be?" said Katie.

"You two are really naïve," said Roger. "They couldn't care less about us. Typical. We've done them a service. Dave and I last night, we probably saved them from a very nasty death."

"And me," said Katie.

"And are we thanked? Are we heck as like? First chance they get, they're off. These people are all the same."

"Gwen's not," said Katie. "She's lovely."

"Well, she's not much older than we are," said Roger, unlocking the Metro. "But she'll go the way of the rest."

"What way's that, then?" said Dave.

"*Horrible* crew: *me, me, me* all the time – they think they're God, the lot of them. Fighting like rats in a cage the moment something goes wrong. I wish they *would* all kill each other. Good riddance."

"You can't count Hugo in that," said Katie. "He never knew what was going on. He wasn't at their secret meeting."

"He's all right, is Hugo," said Dave. "You'd never think he was a world-famous composer."

Roger sat in the driver's seat.

"I'm sitting in the back with Katie," said Dave.

"Suit yourself," said Roger.

They were clear of the village before he spoke again.

"All that business last night," he said. "It doesn't add up. Nobody's asked whether the person who came to see Hugo on Wednesday night, the thief in the day and the arsonist in the Bimmer last night could all be the same person."

"Bill Weston's Hugo's *friend*," said Katie.

Roger gave a short, bitter laugh.

"They're *all* Hugo's friends," he said. "If I had friends like Hugo's I'd go off and be a monk."

"It was surely a coincidence that Weston was in Hugo's village on Wednesday night," said Katie.

"It's no more a coincidence than everything else in the business." Roger was nearly shouting. "He was *waiting* for Hugo. He knew *exactly* when he'd be there. And he fed Hugo all that stuff about Fiona Tankerton."

"Don't you think that's true?" said Dave.

"It may be for all I know. What worries me is *why* he was on hand just like that to tell Hugo. He could pretend to leave, double back, and give Hugo a tap on the head – just enough to lay him out, not enough to really hurt him – while he ransacks the house for the one thing that's of no conceivable use to anyone else. No, I reckon Weston's part of it all."

"OK, let's assume you're right," said Dave. "Was he *really* going to burn the place down? That's mad."

"*Think*," said Roger. "This person's done two things which are very calculated – minimum force, you might

159

say. Then he tries something way over the top, gets caught in the act and runs off like a lunatic. Jekyll in the morning, Hyde at night. Why?"

"How should I know?" said Dave.

"Something happened to make him," said Roger. "When he saw us he was rattled. He couldn't think straight. He ran off like a frightened rabbit. Not much calculation there. I reckon he thought things were going wrong."

"Such as?" said Katie.

"You two are really thick sometimes," said Roger. "You haven't already forgotten what happened yesterday, have you?"

"You mean Stubbs trying to kill me and then killed himself?"

"Exactly. The Bimmer man and Stubbs are part of all this. But only part. There's someone behind them, keeping it all going."

Katie remembered her vision: the spider at the web's heart.

"But Stubbs is dead," Roger went on. "They didn't expect that. You're asking too many questions and doing too much thinking, even if you need me through the difficult bits. The Bimmer man's contacted. He's told what's happened. He flips. He tries something really stupid. And now he's been caught, he's probably scared stiff of his controller. I bet I'm right."

"But why burn Hugo's house down?"

"With Katie in it, remember," said Roger.

"Impossible," said Katie. "How could he *know* I was in it?"

"He was told," said Roger. "Mobile phones – dead easy."

"But nobody knew where I was," Katie said. Then a thought occurred to her. She turned to Dave. "You didn't leave the programme with my message on it lying around, did you?"

Dave pointed to the dashboard.

"There it is," he said.

"Then there's no way the Bimmer man could have known," Katie said.

"Ah well, the best theories always have a flaw," said Roger.

Getting through London to the Hall of Residence took a long time. When Roger finally parked the Metro it was nearly midday. They found Frank Thurlow waiting for them in the entrance. Liz was with him.

"To say I am angry would be a severe understatement," he said. "I am incandescent with rage."

The three shuffled uneasily.

"I'd like to send you all home now and never let you come near me or my orchestra again. But you have a powerful friend. You can thank Hugo that you're playing this evening."

He turned on his heel and left. Before she followed, Liz spoke.

"You shouldn't have done what you did," she said. "You know Frank expects complete loyalty from his orchestra." She looked at Roger and Dave. "I wondered why you were so interested last night in where Hugo lived."

She left them and caught up with Frank. Roger looked triumphant.

"See?" he said. "There doesn't have to be a flaw in what I said. Someone could have heard and put two and two together. The Bimmer man *knew* Katie was there."

"OK," said Katie. "Who heard you?"

"Liz was there," he replied. "And Arthur Armitage. Sam's mum told us where to go. There were others around who could have heard."

"And Fiona Tankerton was talking to Gwen before we left," said Katie. "I'm *sure* Gwen told her we were going somewhere. I don't think she said where, though."

"She could work it out," said Dave. "It depends on how well she knows Gwen."

"So there's a lot who could blow our cover," said Roger.

"But which one?" said Dave.

"I need a shower," said Katie. "We'll think about it over something to eat before the rehearsal."

The hot water was blissful. Katie let the grime and sweat of the last twenty-four hours wash off her. The impulsive moment when she had stood up and followed Stubbs seemed weeks ago. But how much further forward were they? Well, not very. Things didn't fit. She needed some blinding revelation to make the pattern snap into place, so she could say: "I should have known that all along."

If Roger was right, who could have told the BMW man that she had gone to Hugo's? Fiona? But if the story Bill Weston told Hugo was right, and if both the first and last victims sharing the name of Stubbs was not just another of the staggering coincidences which she had by now learnt to distrust, then that was impossible. No murderer, surely, would co-operate with the brother of a victim. More likely murder him as well.

A grim thought came. Stubbs was found dead four floors below Fiona's flat. Could she have done it?

Who else had Roger mentioned?

Liz? No, she could have nothing to do with it. Among the musical adults, she was the one outsider: she hadn't been to the Conservatoire; she didn't know Hugo or Fiona. Frank was the boss who had set up the county's commission to Hugo, and Liz was there because she worked with him.

Arthur Armitage? Nice old man – crusty old twerp. Discount him.

Sam's mum? Well, Mrs Belling *was* connected. She'd been at the Conservatoire when the original trouble happened and she was here now – the one link between past and present who wasn't obviously involved. But, Katie reasoned, a link not obviously involved was exactly what they were looking for.

No, surely not. It couldn't be that the mother of a friend of hers was masterminding a series of murders?

Yes, but – did anything else happen to her all those years ago at the Conservatoire? What had Hugo said about Julian Stubbs? "He had more girlfriends than you've had hot dinners." What if Sam's mum had been one of them? What if she'd been more than just a girl-friend, had harboured thoughts of revenge over the years and was only now putting them into operation after – yes, of course: *Hugo had given her the key.*

The thought made her shiver. Even so, she must think it.

Who had Stubbs met in the museum yesterday? A woman in light blue. Did Sam's mum wear light blue yesterday? Did *anyone?*

Yes, Fiona, in the foyer.

That meant *nothing.* Even so, Katie hoped fervently the woman in the museum was Fiona and not Sam's mum, even if it made nonsense of her theories. What Sam would go through if her theories were right made her shudder to imagine! Because another implication had dawned on her, which she suppressed before she could find words for it.

But if what Weston told Hugo was true, then Fiona probably *was* the woman in the museum. If Stubbs made a secret rendezvous to meet Fiona, that didn't mean they were working together. And if they were – well, why should Stubbs the armed robber have anything to do with Stubbs the talented music student?

Say, though, that Weston was lying. Then the woman in the museum wasn't Fiona. So who was it? Sam's mum?

Round and round, round and round it all went. Even so, it needed just a little skew in her thoughts to sort it out, to make it clear as day. She was *sure* of that.

Katie had gone into the shower feeling a wreck. Half an hour later she was in the cafeteria looking good and feeling great. She joined Dave and Roger in the queue.

"Perhaps we've nearly cracked it," she said.

To be back on the first desk of the cellos, to be part of a large and accomplished body of people working like a well-oiled machine, to be in this most beautiful of concert halls with the staggering acoustics – all these things made Katie forget everything that had smothered her over the last twenty-four hours. She lost herself in the music as Frank took them through their final run-through.

This afternoon, only Mrs Belling, Arthur Armitage, Liz, Hugo, Gwen and a few members of the Citadel Centre staff were there to listen. But this evening, stalls and circle would be crowded with an appreciative audience, wondering if the players they heard would one day return there, gracing the PPO of London and orchestras like it, carrying music on for another generation.

Well, if Hugo had his way, they'd never hear *Variations on a Folk Song Theme* again.

Frank had conducted the *Enigma Variations* and taken Gwen through the Shostakovich Concerto. Liz was plainly pleased by the way the orchestra had responded to her in the Brahms.

Then Hugo came to the rostrum.

"Tonight is the very last performance of this piece," he said. "Make it special."

And as Hugo lifted his baton and Katie waited, bow poised, she realized that things had to come to a head that night; that very soon now all the questions might be answered and that whatever else, she *must not* let her concentration slip.

16

Frank Thurlow sat in the eighth row and listened. Hugo was extracting lovely sounds from the orchestra. Yes, in spite of everything, the tour had been a triumph. Musically, it had been marvellous. He could not remember a better County Youth Orchestra. And who had he to thank for that? Well, himself, of course. Frank knew he was no genius like his old friend Hugo, but he was not one to underestimate his own abilities. He looked to his left where Liz, having wound down after conducting the Brahms and giving a little pep talk, was walking down the aisle towards him. Yes, Liz as always had been a tower of strength. He remembered her disbelief when he said he would approach the great Hugo Malvern. Well, there was enough of the schoolboy still in him to feel a little glee in that triumph.

And Hugo's new work composed specially for them was wonderful. Nothing that had happened since should detract from that. He knew what a buzz the kids got from playing it. A pity about all that other stuff. Yes, it was terrible that all these figures from his past had died or disappeared, but what had it to do with him? Laura, Gerry – there was no connection between them and this tour. He *would not* believe it. That Hugo had been so distracted – and the excellent Gwen on his account – was unfortunate and worrying, but it had not spoilt the tour.

Besides, every cloud had a silver lining. Because of Laura's murder, Gerry's disappearance and the sad but *surely* coincidental business concerning Alicia Vernon, the orchestra had received a lot of publicity. *YOUNG ORCHESTRA DOGGED BY FATAL COINCIDENCE* ran the headline in the *Independent*. *MUSICAL SCARES* said the *Sun*. Whatever else, a full house was guaranteed for tonight's concert. Some, no doubt, would come to see if anything happened to whoever F.T. proved to be. Well, Frank could answer that now. If F.T. was Frank Thurlow, *nothing*. And if it was Fiona Tankerton, she would be sitting in the second row in a complimentary seat Frank had been happy to give her for old times' sake. What a surprise to find her waiting outside the theatre last night. He never thought to speak to such a star again, especially as he only saw her as a shadowy but awesome figure in his student days. Only the likes of Hugo really knew her. And Ken.

Yes, Ken. His friend and Hugo's. He was stopped from discounting the disturbances of this week only because of memories of what had happened to Ken. Those long gone days did often come into his mind; during this week they had returned with a vengeance.

And now some of his players had got involved. He had been furious with Raggett and the Summers girl on Wednesday for seeing the police. Ginny Belling should have known better than to encourage them. And for them to slope off last night with Roger Curle – it defied belief. If it hadn't been for Hugo, they would have been back home by now, sadder but wiser.

Still, that might have been an over-reaction. After all, the police were taking the whole thing seriously. Especially after yesterday's death. An inspector and two sergeants had held long conversations with him, Liz and the Citadel Centre staff. Police would mingle with the public tonight at the centre. They would watch every-thing, but he hoped they would like the music as well.

No, nothing would spoil tonight's final concert.

By now, Liz was sitting next to him.

"Cheer up, Frank," she whispered. "This tour's nearly finished. It's time to think about the Christmas concerts."

Frank jumped up from his seat the moment the last chords of the variation *To F.T.* died away. He joined Hugo as he gave the orchestra his last comments, con-gratulations and advice to enjoy the piece for the last time that night, then he spoke himself.

"You've done wonders. In some ways we've had a bad time this week. None of it was our fault. I've been angry with two or three of you. We'll forget that now, just as we'll forget all the trouble that seems to have followed us wherever we've gone. Because, musically, this is the best summer tour I've ever done and tonight's concert in such a terrific hall is going to be this orchestra's great high point. Remember that and *savour every moment*. Good luck and look forward to the curry supper!"

With that, he walked away.

Roger muttered to Katie. "I reckon there's more than music and curry to savour," he said.

The same four who had sat outside by the fountains the day before were eating together in the cafeteria at the Hall of Residence together with Andy, Dave's colleague on the trombones.

"So what can we do?" said Katie. "We know there are two possible victims called F.T. and they're both here in the Citadel Centre. One's conducting and one lives here."

"Fiona Tankerton will be in the audience," said Samantha. "My mum told me. And there'll be police watching."

Katie and Dave looked at each other. Nobody but them and Roger knew Fiona could have been the original killer. Nor would anyone know Ginny Belling had drawn suspicion to herself.

"So we do nothing," said Andy. "What are the police for?"

"It's different now," said Katie. "The other victims have been miles away. Now, everybody who's had anything to do with it is here under the same roof."

"So what's it to be?" said Andy. "Pistol shots from the audience? Poisoned darts through blowpipes? Do me a favour!"

"What about the Bimmer man?" said Roger. "Where's he?"

"See?" said Katie. "The police don't know everything."

"Shouldn't you tell them, then?" said Andy.

"What's to tell?" said Dave. "If he's Hugo's mate Weston, everybody will know. If he isn't, there's not much to go on except the white Bimmer."

"Probably stolen," said Roger.

"All we can do is keep our eyes open," said Katie.

"All we can do," said Samantha, "is play as well as we know how. This is my last concert as leader and I'm not having any of you ruining it for me."

Suddenly, Katie could not look Samantha in the eyes.

"Not much chance of that," said Roger. "Let's face it, we haven't got a clue what's going to happen."

They were ready to file out into the hall. The boys on this warm night looked casual but smart in white shirts and black trousers; the girls cool in long dresses. Frank had spoken to them for the last time: his usual exhortation to concentrate and enjoy.

Hugo was not to be seen. Liz and Gwen stood together close to Katie. When Frank had finished, Gwen stepped forward.

"Katie," she whispered. "Will you do me a favour? I've got some invitation cards here I'd like you to give out. They're from Fiona. She's giving a little party on the roof garden after the concert."

She showed Katie a small wad of white cards.

"This isn't exactly the ideal time," said Katie.

"I'm sorry," Gwen replied. "The box-office manager's only just given them to me. Someone asked him to."

Katie looked at the top card: *Fiona Tankerton requests the pleasure of your company on the Roof Garden at 10.30 p.m. tonight.*

"Who else is going?" she said doubtfully.

"I am," said Gwen. "Frank, Liz, Hugo, Ginny Belling and you four to represent the rest. Samantha, you, Dave and Roger."

"But we're the ones who know most about what's going on," said Katie, feeling alarmed. "How can she know that? Why does she want us there?"

"She probably remembers you from last night," Gwen replied.

Katie felt a sudden welling of doubt. "But she doesn't know the others," she said. "Remember what Hugo told us about her."

"Who's to say that's true?" said Gwen. "Anyway, there's safety in numbers. She can't do the lot of us in. Besides, if both F.T.s have survived till then, everything must be OK. I for one am going to forget all this and just enjoy myself. You should do the same."

Yes, why not? One reason came at once.

"But we're all supposed to be having a curry together after the concert. It's all arranged."

"Don't worry," said Gwen. "You'll get both."

Fair enough, Katie thought, walking out with the rest. She left the cards in her cello case: they could wait until the interval.

Stepping into the air-conditioned hall with its wood-panelled walls glowing golden and the raked seats full of expectant people gave Katie a thrill of anticipation. And more than that: after all the alarms of the past thirty-six hours, moving into the light, sitting down and tuning her beloved cello gave her a feeling of peace and continuity. *This* was what it was all about, not distractions about a murderous quarrel between people she neither knew nor really cared about. Perhaps Roger had been right that morning when Hugo and Gwen had roared away together in the Porsche.

The delicious sound of a whole orchestra tuning up was over. Samantha as leader was walking to her place, her honey-gold hair glowing like the walls of the hall. Applause rolled like a gentle sea, died away, then returned as Frank entered to conduct Elgar's *Enigma Variations*.

In this magical hall, Katie felt at one with the music even more than before. Elgar's *Nimrod* variation – expansive, soaring, yearning, inexpressibly sad – seemed like a lament for all those dead whom she never knew: Julian, Rosalie, Ken, Laura, possibly Alicia. And those she did know, however slightly – Gerald Swordblade perhaps, her stalker and near-killer Stubbs definitely. Could she imagine a lament for him? Why not? People were dead or missing who shouldn't be. And *Nimrod* underlined her sadness for them.

But there was more to the *Enigma Variations* than *Nimrod*. By the time Frank had led them to the rumbustious ending she felt, as always, exhilarated.

The piece was over. Now applause surged from the steeply raked seats like Atlantic breakers driving on to the shore. Frank took his bow and the orchestra stood to acknowledge the clapping. Frank left and the grand piano was brought into place. Soon he reappeared, leading Gwen. She looked, Katie thought, as composed and beautiful as ever, her long black hair pouring in ringlets over her shoulders, her smile unforced and warm. Where was the worried, agitated person of the night before?

Shostakovich's Second Piano Concerto had, to Katie, never sounded better. Gwen showed exactly why Hugo thought she would become one of the great pianists. When it was over she stood to receive the tumultuous applause and Katie thought she seemed transfigured, on another plane. She felt sudden envy. Was it possible her cello would take her to such heights? Now she was convinced that this was what, above all, she wanted. In that moment, her life's ambition crystallized. But another question came. Would she take Dave with her?

The interval was here: members of the orchestra talked noisily over coffee. Katie went to the chosen four with Fiona's invitation. Each took it almost without noticing, although Samantha looked pleased and Roger said, "What about my curry, then?"

Frank's voice carried over the chattering and stilled it.

"Anybody seen Liz?" he called. "I don't want her missing just before Brahms."

Just then the door opened and Liz slipped in.

"Sorry, Frank," she said. "I had to make a phone call."

"Oh," said Frank. "Well, sorry I drew attention to you."

Not for the first time, he reflected on how he wished Liz led a life outside her music and her job. Her previous husband had treated her badly, but surely *someone* ought to be here to support her in her small conducting triumph?

Liz, though, needed no sympathy. She was her brisk, efficient self as she used the lull for a few last words.

"Come on, all of you," she said. "Make this really count. Our last effort for a while at Brahms."

"Leaving Liszt till afterwards," a tympanist called out.

"I didn't hear that," Liz said as she opened the door and watched them as they filed out for the last time on this the summer tour.

The *Academic Festival Overture* by Johannes Brahms just seemed to get better every time they played it. Often, as Liz guided them expertly through the lively student tunes and bustling rhythms, Katie reflected that she was probably the best musician of the lot of them.

Now she had left the rostrum for the last time. The orchestra was seated again and tuning up ready for Hugo.

And here he was – tall, elegant and easy-moving, with a lock of wavy hair falling over his forehead, tail coat and white tie worn carefully casual. Katie remembered her first sight of him and what she had thought. Yes, he really was *dreamy*. And was it make-up or the lighting that had made last night's livid bruise disappear?

He stood, smiling encouragement. Then he brought them in to the beginning of his Theme and Variations. Katie lifted her eyes to watch him – and in that moment caught sight of Fiona Tankerton sitting, listening intently, in the middle of the second row.

No, nothing untoward had happened so far. Perhaps, after all, it never would.

* * *

The two biggest audiences of the evening at the Citadel Centre — one in the theatre, one in the concert hall — were safely where they should be. Few people walked the levels or the foyers, browsed in the bookstores or sat in the bars. Outside, as darkness came and the fountains played unwatched, two dark figures saw each other and met. They now sat at the very table from which Katie had risen the day before to follow a man whose life would not last out the afternoon.

Theme, Autumn, By Cutler's Mere, To L.M. Katie played them as music, thought of them as the retelling of a painful story. *Winter, On Granden Fell, To G.S.* Another story, this one unfinished. Would Gerald Swordblade ever be found? *Summer, In Carteret Woods, To A.V.* Katie recalled the shock of seeing the newspaper report and putting two and two together so unexpectedly. What end was there to *that* story? With Fiona Tankerton in front of her and Frank Thurlow visible at the side of the stage hanging on to every note, how could there be an ending?

"*So you're here.*"

"*I've been guided well.*"

"*No change of mind?*"

"*Why should there be? I believe you. It's time this thing was done. It's been a cancer for too long.*"

"*And no regrets about what I did to convince you and bring you here?*"

"*Many. But I'll forgive you for now. There may still be scores to settle when this is all over.*"

175

"Then come with me. We have work to do."

The two figures left the table and slipped away towards the lift leading to the upper level of the Citadel Centre.

Summer. A warm, joyous piece blazing with golden brass and bright with lush woodwind and soaring strings. In this rich music Hugo's world came to full fruition. Katie loved this variation. But always when she played it came a nagging thought: after such a shining statement as this, what could possibly succeed it?

The lift doors opened. Up here, three levels above the place where even now the orchestra was playing its heart out, there was an eerie quiet. To one side was an empty exhibition gallery: its stark photographs from Bosnia were at this moment unviewed. To another, behind a glass wall, was a meeting room in the form of a palm court, the trees still, brooding, silhouetted in indirect light. But neither place was the destination of these two. They walked further, up steps to a yet higher level.

They reached a door which opened at their touch and emerged into light and a fresh, warm breeze. They stood on a floor of brick and York Stone cobbles. Round them sighed flowers, shrubs and small trees. They were on the roof garden.

Three white-coated people were laying out a table for a small buffet. They turned at the sound of the door.

"You can't come here," said one. "This is a private party."

"That's all right," said one of the two intruders, stepping into the light. "I'm a friend of the host."

The attendant looked at the face now revealed.

"Of course," he said. *"Now I see who you are. Sorry. But you can't be too careful."*

"Quite so," was the answer.

"We were worried about you, sir," said the attendant. *"I'm glad to see you here."*

Around London was busy, fast, energetic. Brass blared. Dave always had a terrific time in this variation. The original theme was almost lost in the array of noise and life. The percussion section had extra things to do: blowing whistles, banging gongs and bells, sounding horns and hooters. Yet little phrases on the strings – especially the cellos, which pleased Katie because she loved shaping them against the cacophony – made sure that Little Musgrave was never completely forgotten, swamped by the traffic.

But the sudden jumping chord which cut the variation off into complete silence to prepare for *To F.T.* left everyone temporarily limp before they gathered up their strength for the last push.

"Don't mind us," said one of the intruders. *"Carry on. We'll wait over here."*

They withdrew to the edge and looked over the balustrade, down to the fountains far below – and then away, beyond. One way lay St Paul's, Canary Wharf, the City Airport, the River Thames winding towards the Essex marshes. To the other side, the Telecom Tower twinkled, Centre Point glowed slightly and the lights of the West End gleamed. London stretched below them. But they did not seem interested in the view. Rather, they were noting the positions of the fire escapes.

"A fitting end?" said one.

"Indeed, yes," said the other.

To F.T. Hugo's new work wound its way to the end. When she first encountered it, Katie had wondered how, after the overpowering energy of the two previous variations, Hugo would provide something memorable for the finale. Apart from the theme itself, the last variation was the clearest rendition of the Little Musgrave tune in the whole work. But its character was changed: now it moved calmly, serenely, taken up by all the sections of the orchestra in turn, to the accompaniment of solid, impressive chords which moved unstoppably. Katie always thought of a great ship, after a long, storm-tossed voyage, finally moving majestically into harbour.

As the great concerted chords moved to their climax and died away, as Katie made the final flourish of her bow against tensed strings, as the audience burst into clapping and cheering, she reflected – if F.T. was Frank, there were depths to him she never suspected. It *must* be Fiona.

The table was laid: the attendants had gone. Where the intruders stood was very quiet.

"Now we wait," said one.

17

Katie by now hardly bothered with the swelling applause, or the sight of Hugo bowing and expansively gesturing to the orchestra to stand. She rose with the rest almost automatically. For, in this week of bizarre happenings, the most bizarre, she was sure, was about to take place. If Fiona Tankerton, underneath her fame and her brilliance, was a killer many times over, why should she end her week's work with a party for the very people who suspected her most?

Or was the whole thing completely innocent because Fiona had nothing to do with the deaths? In which case, was she unwittingly setting up a stage for her *own* death as F.T. In front of guests? That would be incredible.

The applause finished. The orchestra filed off stage. The concerts and the music were gone, whipped away from her life. Now – was she going up to the roof garden for a pleasant chat? Or to watch – and be part of – the last act of the drama?

Winding down immediately afterwards, Samantha wished no invitation had come her way. She sighed for the long, curry-bearing tables in the Hall of Residence. And what some said when they heard just a few were going to a roof garden party with a star was quite upsetting.

Oh, *why* did all this have to happen and *ruin* her great tour?

Frank, too, was angry with the invitation.

"I've a duty to my kids," he stormed at Liz. "I don't care how famous she is or if I knew her once. We *always* have a big supper after the last concert. And I'm always at it."

"I know," said Liz. "But it's a kind thought and we mustn't snub her. We'll just put in a quick appearance."

"If you're worried about clearing the hall and packing up," said Arthur Armitage, "forget it."

"We'll see to all that," said Anita Smith. "And we'll get everybody down to the supper. It will all be ready for you when you arrive. What else are the Friends of the Orchestra for? You two and Ginny go off and enjoy yourselves. You deserve it."

"But she's invited kids as well," said Frank. "What's the stupid woman thinking of? There's such a thing as loyalty."

The floodlit roof garden was lovely. The four orchestra

members tagged along with Gwen to the lift and up the stairs. Frank was already there, impatiently looking at his watch. He muttered to Samantha as they stepped out into the open air, "We'll pay our respects and be out of here the moment we can."

But the buffet did look super, the panoramic view of London was wonderful and Fiona Tankerton herself stood looking so welcoming and expansive and – amazing for a possible serial killer – so *nice*, that Katie realized it would be quite difficult to leave. Even Frank's anger seemed to die while Liz looked positively radiant, Katie thought, seeing her talking and laughing with Ginny Belling, the subdued lighting reflecting off the sheeny silk of her evening gown.

Roger sidled up, a paper plate piled with cocktail sausages and mushroom vol-au-vents, and whispered conspiratorially.

"I wonder if Hercule Poirot's here to tell us who did it?"

"No chance," Katie replied. "Fiona wouldn't invite people to her own downfall. This is just a nice way to end the tour. It was lovely of her to ask us."

"You reckon?" said Roger and went off to fill his glass.

Katie was left alone. She looked round. Fiona stood near her, also for a moment alone, looking out over London. A piston-engined plane flew overhead, coming in to land at London City Airport to the east. As the noise died away, Katie thought: *I'll speak to her*. She felt trepidation as she approached the great singer.

"Miss Tankerton?" she said.

Fiona turned and looked at her.

"I know you," she said. "You were with Gwen last night, outside the theatre. You played very well tonight, all of you."

"Thank you," said Katie. An awkward silence for a second, then: "It's lovely of you to set this party up and invite us to it."

Fiona looked puzzled.

"Me?" she said. "What gave you the idea that *I* invited you? I thought *you* invited *me*."

"Your name's on the invitations," said Katie.

"Let me see," said Fiona.

Katie handed her the little card. Fiona studied it, her lips pursed. Then she said, "Well, it doesn't matter if someone's playing a little trick. Let's enjoy it, shall we?"

But suddenly Katie couldn't enjoy it. This was more than a little trick. Fiona obviously decided she could not let the other guests labour under a misapprehension. She stood by the buffet table and called for quiet.

"Listen, everybody," she said. "This is slightly embarrassing. It seems you all think I invited you up here. Well, this is so nice that I wish I had. But I'm sorry to disappoint you. You have someone else to thank. I wonder who the mystery person is?"

In the dark, by the fire escape, the two figures listened.

"Time," said one. "Let's go."

There was silence after Fiona spoke, then an embarrassed giggle.

Suddenly, all the lights went out.

This is getting a habit, thought Katie.

There were shouts of alarm and then Frank's voice sounded. "Is one of you kids playing the fool?"

As quickly, the lights were back on. Katie, like everybody else, blinked and looked round.

There were extra guests at the party.

Two men stood there. They were smartly dressed in dark suits and white shirts as if ready to play in the orchestra. One had a short, light topcoat slipped over his shoulders. Amazed gasps echoed round the roof garden as people took in who they were.

Hugo knew one of them: a tall, middle-aged man with a lean, sardonic face – the one with the topcoat. "Bill," he said. "Bill Weston. What are you doing here?"

But it was the other person who brought out the really profound shock. For standing in front of them was Sir Gerald Swordblade.

In the darkness, more people had arrived on the roof garden unseen. They stood unobserved behind shrubs, waiting.

"Gerry, you're not dead!" cried Gwen.

Hugo looked at him, unable to speak.

"Oh, no," said Gerry. "I'm spared to fight another day. I'm here to tell you a story. Bear with me, it's quite long. I'm back to settle an old score. I'm here for the justice I've vainly sought for nearly twenty years."

The warm night breeze ruffled the hair of the silent listeners. Hugo, Frank, Fiona, Liz, Gwen – all looked intently at him. So did Katie and the rest. What final revelations would he bring?

"You know what happened years ago. You know how

my wife died a terrible death and how a bright young student died with her. And I know what some people here thought – that I killed them, that I crept into my own holiday cottage as they slept, trapped them inside and then burnt the house down round them. That was a terrible accusation. Nobody made it out loud, though I know full well many wanted to. But some of us swore an oath, did we not, that we would never speak a word of what we thought. For other suspicions were swirling around that night the six of us met. But I *did not do* that terrible thing. I was angry enough to – but I did not. Perhaps I wasn't as grief-stricken as I should have been, but I did not murder my wife."

"Gerry," said Frank. "Perhaps nobody did it. Perhaps it *was* accidental. The police thought so."

Gerry looked at him.

"Dear Frank," he said. "Would that it were so. But you had a grief of your own very soon after. Your good friend Ken Vanstone. I remember you three friends so well. Hugo, Frank and Ken – The Three Musketeers. Suddenly the Three Stooges."

"Ken was mugged." Frank's voice sounded strangled. "The police never found out who did it."

Gerry looked at him again, this time pityingly.

"I repeat, Frank – *would that he were*."

Frank was silent.

"So the years went by," Gerry said. "I've had a successful life. I achieved my great ambition: Principal of the Royal National Conservatoire. I was even knighted for my services to music. But I know many people think I played foully for it, while *I* believe someone is out there who *really* knows, who *was* there that first, terrible night – and who was there that second terrible night when Ken was murdered."

"And I think I know who you mean, Gerry," said Hugo.

Gerry continued.

"But sleeping dogs lie and life went on. Until strange news came to me. Hugo, my prize pupil, the greatest product of my teaching, was writing a new work to a commission. I saw Hugo regularly, but the news came to me secondhand. Why didn't my old friend tell me himself? Then I saw what he was writing – variations on *Little Musgrave and Lady Barnard*. Hugo, I am not a fool. I *knew* what you were saying. I saw that the story of Little Musgrave mimicked perfectly what you thought had happened. Now I had a dilemma. Should I go to you and say, 'Hugo, you're wrong'? Well, while I waited, you came to me. Last Sunday – six short days ago. Already it seems a lifetime. You had a wild story of messages and keys and visits by ghosts from the past. And you were full of accusations. Well, Hugo, I was angry with you, I admit it. I came to Wardminster next night to hear your piece and make amends. Did we part on good terms? I hope so. Then away to my holiday – and the dreadful news of Laura's murder and the knowledge that the sleeping dog had woken. There is a fiend walking the earth."

Gwen interrupted.

"Gerry, I tried to warn you that you would be next."

Gerry looked at her.

"Thank you, Gwen," he said. "I got your message when I arrived at my cottage by the fells. But then the beauty of the place, a burst of hard walking, good food, wine and woodsmoke lulled me to sleep. Until I woke and heard the call."

"The call?" said Hugo.

"Yes," said Gerry. "Someone had come to see me. No, Gwen, it was not some cruel killer, hands dripping with the blood of L.M. coming to dispose of G.S. It was a ghost from the past. It was an old friend who had sought me out. Bill Weston, who I thought had faded from my life for ever, came out of the night to tell me all at last."

Every eye turned to the tall man. A tiny thought nudged its way into Katie's mind: *I've seen him before.*

"Go on, Gerry," he said. "This is your story. You tell it."

"Bill came into my living room. We sat for hours while we talked. He reminded me of that strange evening when we met: him, Laura, Alicia, Fiona, me. The tensions, the unspoken accusations. My wife and her lover horribly dead. I looked round. *They all believed I did it, outraged at my wife's treachery and my pupil's presumption.* I looked at Ken, snivelling with fear. Yes, he was the page in the ballad. But I was *not* Lord Barnard. Was there another Lord Barnard in the room? Had Ken told someone else? Someone who could be more enraged even than me?"

He stopped and looked round his audience.

"Bill told me that there was. Things that night were not as they appeared. We all swore we would never breathe a word against each other, we would always support each other. Why? Because we thought we were on a higher plane than other mortals, that our talents put us above the laws of ordinary people. We could not be distracted by the crimes and jealousies of the petty world outside. But perhaps some of us had things to hide."

Silence again. Gerry looked at Hugo.

"The night Rosalie and Julian died," he said, "I was not at the cottage. But I was not where I should have been either – and I never wanted it known where I was. Especially, Hugo, by you."

"Go on, Gerry," said Hugo.

"Hugo, while you were in hospital, I was with Alicia."

Hugo said nothing for a moment. Then, quietly: "I never suspected. She never said. It doesn't matter now, Gerry."

"Thank you," said Gerry. "So you see there were some people in the room who wanted no eyes prying into where they were the night of the deaths. But who were they besides me?"

Suddenly, Gerry looked Fiona full in the face.

"Fiona, I thought that you were protecting me when you called on us to swear an oath. No matter that I had not done what you thought I had: I certainly needed protecting. But Bill has told me the truth. *You* went to the cottage with Ken; *you* caused the death of my wife and a fine student."

Now everybody's eyes were on Fiona. *So Hugo heard right; Bill Weston told the truth*, thought Katie.

But Fiona did not flinch from the combined gaze.

"Anything else while you're about it, Gerry?" she said. The only word which could describe her voice, Katie thought, was *contemptuous*. Until that moment, Gerald Swordblade had been calm, his voice level and measured. Now he changed.

"You killed them, Fiona," he shouted. "You trapped them, set the house alight and left them to die. Then you did more. You murdered poor Ken because he was weak and was going to spill the beans on you. And when you heard that Hugo had written something which would make people look back on it all, question their consciences, wonder what *really* happened, you started on a final quest to silence each one, once and for all. Poor, innocent Laura's dead. The missing Alicia will make no dramatic reappearance as I did. You are an evil woman, Fiona Tankerton, and I am only sorry it has taken me so long to find out."

Fiona only laughed. Her voice was full of scorn.

"And I'm supposed to have done the job on my own?" she said. "My word, Gerry, I must be a strong one. So many murders, all by myself. All those years ago and this week as well. And I hardly left London."

"Oh, no, Fiona, you had an accomplice. I agree, it wouldn't make sense if you hadn't. Julian's brother, Ronald Stubbs. Just out of prison, with a lot of scores to settle and a need for money. A willing partner. But it came to an end yesterday afternoon, didn't it? When you killed him, bundled him over your balcony to his death. What happened, Fiona? Did he demand too much money? Was he scared and threatening to go to the police? Was he blackmailing you?"

Fiona spoke with heavy sarcasm.

"Is that all, Gerry?"

"It's finished, Fiona," said Gerry. "The police are here."

The people who had entered unseen when the lights went out moved forward from behind the shrubs – an inspector, a sergeant and a WPC. They had listened unobserved.

"I see," said Fiona. "So our mysterious party-giver invited us all here for a show trial. Well, all accused have a right to their defence. There's no sense in resisting these officers. They can judge for themselves what I have to say to them. But before I'm taken away, just listen to *this*, Gerald Swordblade."

With surprising agility she leapt nimbly on to the buffet table. Now she faced her accusers and everyone else – tall, imposing, statuesque. Her voice poured down on them with all the strength which had for years thrilled audiences.

"Yes, little blabbermouth Ken told me about Julian and Rosalie, just as he told you. And, yes, I was angry and, yes, I made him come down with me that night to the cottage where they were. All I wanted to do was confront them, to make Julian squirm, to embarrass Rosalie. I wasn't going to kill anybody. I *couldn't*. Well, we watched the house, Ken and I. We knew they were in there. We saw lights on, we saw them go off. We waited until I judged it time to burst in. I had a key – you should be careful what you leave lying around, Gerry. But then we saw a glow in a downstairs room. Something was on fire. It spread quickly. What should we do? Rush in and perform rescues which might not work and only draw attention to ourselves? No. Best slip away and ring the Fire Brigade as quickly as we could. So that was what we did. Not until next morning did we know that Rosalie and Julian were dead. *But nobody meant it to happen.* The police were right. The fire was accidental, a cigarette end smouldering on man-made furniture fabric, fumes and flame spreading in a flash. They had no chance. Neither would we if we'd gone in. *Of course* I wanted no one to know where I'd been. But as for the rest, Gerry – well, do you think I've felt good over all these years about what I did that night? No, I've gone through hell over it. But for anyone to think that *I* would kill Ken or fear any revelations Laura or Alicia might make – well, it's the biggest, most ludicrous fantasy I have ever heard. Someone is playing an elaborate and very nasty game with both of us, Gerry, and we ought to think very carefully about who it is."

Gerry looked nonplussed. He turned speechlessly to Bill.

"Fiona's last performance," said Bill. "But not quite her best. Gerry, we've both been your friends. One of us still is. We can't both be right. But I'm the one who's told the truth."

The inspector stepped forward. "Fiona Tankerton, it is my duty…"

Once again the little thought gnawed away in Katie's mind:

I've seen Bill Weston before.

The police had gone, taking a strangely compliant Fiona with them. A cowed, shocked group of people remained.

"This is incredible," said Frank. "They can't make it stick. They must only want Fiona for questioning."

"I'm afraid they'll do more than just question her," said Gerry. "I spent some time with the police this morning, telling them what I knew from Bill."

"Yes, what happened to you?" said Gwen. "Seeing your car being lifted out of the water on TV made us sure you were dead."

"That was Bill's idea," said Gerry. "If I disappeared, leaving my car looking as though it had been dumped, that would rattle Fiona – make her wonder what's happening. Don't worry about the car. A good service on the brakes should sort it out. I would disappear for a while and do a bit of investigating myself, culminating with a visit to the police here. I put up with hours of questioning, convinced them I was right, and together we set up this little charade to trap a killer. And Bill and I met up again this evening in time for the party."

"You could have been done for wasting police time," said Hugo.

"Not when I told them all this," said Gerry.

Now Gerry turned to the whole assembly as if he had organized everything.

"Come on, folks," he said. "Time to go."

"You and Bill will come and share a curry supper with us, won't you?" said Frank. "We can squeeze in two extra chairs."

"Love to," said Bill.

Frank turned away through the door and out of the roof garden as if he couldn't leave it quickly enough. The rest followed. But the four orchestra members found themselves hanging back. They were unhappy. They had listened to everything: this whole extraordinary performance.

"Something's wrong," Dave muttered. "I don't believe a word of it."

"I'm so sad for Fiona," said Samantha. "I just can't believe it."

Katie looked at her. *Better Fiona than your mother*, she thought.

Then she looked to where Bill Weston was talking to Gerry and Hugo as they entered the lift to take them to the lower levels.

I'll place him soon, she thought. *I know I will.*

That was just one of the many questions which were surging round her mind. The biggest, though, was drowning the others. What, after all, would Fiona be accused of – and go on trial for? Of murdering three people years ago. OK, she denied it. Who wouldn't? But let's suppose she did it. She had certainly confirmed being there when the first two died – and was in the company of the third. But after all this time, surely no case could be made for either. Even so, she must have been fearful, years later, that it would all come out. So she got someone – who himself ended up dead – to get a warning to Hugo that something was afoot which scared him rigid. Then she seemed to embark on a programme of getting rid of everyone who had sworn an oath to keep quiet. With Laura Merchant, she started with the least likely, the most innocent – or perhaps Ronald Stubbs travelled to Hedford to do it. Well, if he did, nobody would ever know now. Fiona missed out on the next, which should have been Gerry, but presumably got herself abroad to Amsterdam to do *something* to Alicia – time or confession alone would tell what. Meanwhile, Ronald Stubbs was sitting very obviously in the audience for the concert at Hedford. And then what? Well, that nasty little man ended up spattered over the pavement. And if she hadn't been caught, who would have been next? Gerry? Bill? Hugo?

And all of this – for what? Katie couldn't begin to understand the motives of these people. She had picked up enough about the inner circle and the way they stuck together to know that what Gerry had just said about their talents for music putting them above ordinary mortals was true. It's a funny world, Katie thought. Things which might actually help *EastEnders* stars would finish opera singers for good. If what Fiona did on that first night years ago at the cottage were ever to be known by the world, her life in the public eye would be over.

Well, now it really would be over for this haughty lady as even now she was being grilled by the police. And she had been lured up to the roof garden for this – what had Fiona called it? A show trial.

Katie shuddered. The murderer could only be Fiona, who had seen her with Gwen, who knew she was at Hugo's. It *had* to be.

So why was she so ill at ease?

Everything seemed to hang on who could have known she had gone to Sussex with Gwen so the accomplice in the BMW could at least make a second attempt to silence her at Hugo's house – an accomplice who could *not* be Ronald Stubbs, who by then was in the police morgue. That person *must* be Fiona.

Unless Dave had told someone. He wouldn't, would he? Or had someone overheard him and Roger? Or listened to what they said and put two and two together? And then, like the puppeteer, the spider in the web, got a message through? Who could it be?

Suddenly, she found herself holding her breath, like someone peering into darkness and seeing a blinding white light.

Of course! Forget Fiona. Dave said they got Hugo's address from Ginny Belling, Sam's mum.

Not for the first time, Katie looked at her, blonde hair like her daughter's, laughing with Gerry. She was the one person who had been around years ago when it all started and was here again now it must be ending.

What had Sam said that evening at Wardminster? "He wasn't really my father, you know." No, Sam's real father was a student at the Royal National Conservatoire. Now Katie found herself able to put words to the thought she had tried to smother yesterday. *Julian Stubbs knew Ginny very well indeed. Julian Stubbs was Sam's father. Ginny Belling had over the years harboured thoughts of resentment and revenge on these people. They had blown Julian away and cut short her own career by making her leave the Conservatoire. Only now did she have the chance to put those thoughts into practice.*

Yes, it was falling into place. All these nagging, disturbing visions of the puppeteer, the spider, the controller – Ginny Belling fitted them. She could be in touch all the time: where the orchestra was, where Hugo, Gerry, Gwen were, sending messages by phone or fax or leaving them on answering machines. If you timed it right you could get in touch with anybody anywhere nowadays. *And Ginny Belling could do it.*

And the person she would be in touch with was the man driving the BMW, the dark figure foiled by Dave and Roger from committing the most terrible act of all. *Who was he?*

Oh, this was all too much. How could she carry such a secret alone?

"Cheer up, Katie," said Sam. "It'll soon be curry time."

Katie realized with a shock that they had walked nearly all the way to the Hall of Residence while these thoughts had coursed round her mind.

"It's all over," Sam went on. "You don't have to worry any more."

Katie looked at her and tears blinded her eyes.

18

S am, shocked, looked at Katie.
"What's the matter?"

What should she say? It just wasn't time yet to come
out with her theories. They would destroy Sam in her
hour of triumph. Katie didn't know Sam all that well –
they came from different parts of the county and only
met when the orchestra was together. But she really liked
her and – now that Sam seemed to be hitting it off with
Roger, Katie's companion of the first desk – was seeing
more of her. A burgeoning friendship couldn't be blasted
away like this, surely? And what horror and grief would
Sam suffer?

But Katie had to know more. She chose her words
carefully.

"Did your mother keep in touch with your real
father?"

A look of surprise crossed Sam's face.

"That's a strange thing to come up with now," she said.

"I want to know," Katie replied.

"What business is it of yours?"

"None. I'm sorry. Forget I asked."

"Don't worry. I'll answer. The truth is, I've no idea. I don't even know exactly who my father was. She says one day she'll tell me. Not yet, though. It's too soon after Dad dying. It doesn't matter. I can wait."

"Wouldn't you like to know, though?"

"Why? I've got on all these years without knowing."

I've got to push this a bit harder, Katie thought.

"He might have been a student at the Conservatoire at the same time as your mum," she said.

"He might," said Sam equably. "She'll tell me in her own good time."

And further yet. The next stage could be dangerous.

"He might have been Julian Stubbs."

"*Rubbish!*" Sam answered forcefully. Then, quieter, "What are you getting at?"

"I don't know," Katie said. There was anguish in her voice.

Sam didn't answer. Katie could almost see her mind busy putting two and two together. Then she gave Katie an odd, quizzical look before running to catch up with the adults, taking her mother by the arm and talking brightly.

I've sown a seed in her mind, Katie thought. And she's not happy. Why didn't I keep my big mouth shut? I could lose a friend.

*　　*　　*

Katie did not enjoy her curry. Shouting and laughter swirled round her. Everybody was celebrating the end of a job well done and the lifting of a cloud from over their heads. She couldn't join in.

Dave noticed. He grasped her hand and squeezed it under the table.

"Cheer up, love," he said. "It's nothing to do with us any more. Let the police sort it out."

She leant her head on his shoulder.

"Oh, Dave," she said. "How *can* we?"

She looked further up the table. Sam, pointedly separate from Roger, sat next to her mother as if distancing herself from the rest of the orchestra. As well she might, Katie thought. I've made her think things she wouldn't want to. Hugo and Gwen sat together as well – next to Frank who was at the head of the table, expansive and supremely happy. Bill and Gerry, talking like long-lost brothers, sat next to Hugo. Anita Smith, sitting the other side of Bill, seemed to find everything they said incredibly funny. Opposite them were Liz and Arthur Armitage. There was a sort of adult "high table" and it sounded as raucous as the rest.

The meal was over. Frank rose to his feet. Hugo banged on the table for quiet and Frank spoke.

"Well, we've come to the end," he said. "And a wonderful tour it's been. There are so many people to thank –" and here he embarked on a long list – "and ending, of course, with the person who brought the one thing which made the tour so different – my old friend Hugo Malvern."

The room resounded with cheers and stamping. When

198

order was restored, Frank went on. "This week hasn't been easy for Hugo, or for any of us. I won't go into that now. But I want to thank you – well, *most* of you –" did Katie detect a meaning glance towards her and Dave then? – "for the calm and professional way you've dealt with all these difficulties. And now, as custom demands and inclination insists, the orchestra leader will say a few words. Ladies and gentlemen, I give you the talented, the delectable *Samantha Belling*!"

More roars and cheers. Samantha stood up to speak. She looked diffidently at the throng. Katie noticed she had no notes. Hugo banged on the table again. Everyone was quiet. Samantha's voice came quietly, clearly, from the heart.

"This should have been the greatest week of my life so far," she said. "But it's been spoilt. The ones who spoilt it know who they are." Tears stood in her eyes; her voice shook. "And I won't hear anything bad said about my mother. I love my mum and I'm glad she's been here. She's done nothing wrong and she's got nothing to be ashamed of. So some of you in this room can just shut up."

Now the tears really flowed and Samantha sat down, head in her hands. Ginny Belling put her arm round her shoulders and looked defiantly round the room. Katie wished she could just shrivel up and disappear.

In the embarrassed silence, Gerry spoke.

"Of course," he said. "I knew there was something about you that rang a bell. Now I see the resemblance. Julian was your father, wasn't he?"

An anguished cry came from Ginny Belling. "Gerry,

how *could* you say that in front of everybody?"

Gerry looked shamefaced.

"I'm sorry," he said. "That was so crass of me. But the moment I realized I just couldn't keep it to myself."

Frank stood again, his face creased with confusion. The quiet was broken. Everybody started talking. Curious looks were directed at both Ginny and Sam. Suddenly, Ginny Belling burst out with "I can't stand this!", rose to her feet and ran from the room. Immediately, Sam followed her.

Katie thought: *What have I done?*

Frank spoke quickly, as if to limit the damage.

"Well, I reckon that's about wrapped things up for tonight. I'm sorry it's ended like this. You'd better all get off to bed. It's late."

For a while, people stayed sitting where they were. Then Arthur and Anita stood and one by one the rest followed. Katie felt terrible. More than anything she wanted to find Sam and her mother, to tell them she didn't mean it, that she was out of order. And yet – of everybody there, Ginny Belling had the motive and plenty of opportunity to control events from afar. This *couldn't* be let rest.

"Well, well," said Dave to Katie as they walked out. "What an ending. Tears before bedtime. And there was me stuffed full of running buffet and steaming bowls of curry and thinking it was Christmas every day when you joined Frank's mob."

Katie half heard him. Most of her mind was taken up with worrying about Ginny and Sam. It really did seem possible that...

"Sorry?" she said. Don't snub Dave of all people now, she told herself. It looked as though she might need all the friends she could get.

"I said I thought it was Christmas every day when you played for Frank's mob."

Christmas. A sudden rush of unexpected associations swirled into Katie's mind the moment that word was spoken. Her mind left the problem of Sam and her mother. Yes, it would soon be time to rehearse for the Christmas concerts – if Frank let her stay in the orchestra. Last Christmas had been her first time with the CYO, and she wanted to repeat those magical experiences. But why had she found herself thinking of *this*, now of all times, when there was so much more that was really pressing and urgent? The mind could play weird tricks sometimes.

Suddenly, she saw herself standing outside the rehearsal room at the Music Centre, waiting for her parents to pick her up. Cars drew up all round her, filled up and went. Why should she think of that *now*? What odd process was at work? Why did it somehow *matter*?

Dave spoke again and suddenly she was back with her immediate problem.

"What are you going to do about Sam?" he said.

"What can I do? She won't want to see me now."

"You've got to face her. And she's got to face facts. We're going along to her room to sort it out. Now."

"*No!*" Katie cried.

"Oh, yes we will. And we'll take Roger as well. If anything's going on between him and Sam, he ought to be there."

Yes, Dave was right. Unwillingly, Katie consented, though she felt apprehensive. But finding Roger was not so easy. "Do we have to?" was on the tip of Katie's tongue before they found him making hot drinks with two others in a kitchen on the landing.

He went with them quickly enough. But as Katie explained what she suspected about Sam's mum, his face clouded over.

"I won't listen. That's absolute garbage."

"Then we've got to prove Sam's mum wasn't involved."

"And how are you going to do that?" said Roger.

They had reached Sam's room. It was locked.

"We'll try her mum's, then," said Katie.

"What will we do if they're not there?" said Dave.

Yes, what? Katie had no clear idea. But she would have to make her mind up soon because they were walking down the corridor to Ginny Belling's room.

The door was closed but there was a strip of light showing underneath it.

"Sshh!" said Katie.

Voices came from inside. They were raised, emotional.

"Do you feel good about listening through keyholes?" said Roger.

No, she didn't. But what else could they do?

"I'm off," said Roger, turning to go.

Just then a voice shrilled out clearly through the door. It was Ginny's.

"I *would* have told you! How could I know all this would happen in one week?"

Now all three, including Roger, bent down to the door

and listened intently.

"But, Mum, can't you see how it might look?"

"Of *course* I can. But it's not true. I've nothing to do with these people any more."

Silence. Then came something they couldn't hear. But Katie had a sudden idea of what it was and they all jumped backwards just in time as the door flew open and Sam stood there quivering with anger.

"I *knew* it!" she shouted. "You can't let it rest, can you? Well, you were right about my father. But that's all there is to it. My mum's got nothing to do with any murders. So just – oh, get *out*, will you?"

She looked past Katie and saw Roger standing there, embarrassed and guilty.

"You too, eh?" she said. "Just when I was thinking – oh, go away, the lot of you!"

She turned her back on them and sat on the bed. Her shoulders shook with crying.

"Satisfied, Katie?" said Roger.

This had been a terrible mistake. She turned to go, but Ginny Belling had come forward to the door.

"Wait a minute, Katie," she said.

"Don't talk to them, Mum." Sam's voice was muffled but urgent.

"I must," Ginny replied. Then, "Yes, I know how it must look to you. Julian Stubbs was Sam's father. Oh, I was very young and completely knocked sideways by this romantic violinist. He seemed to me some twentieth-century Paganini. And I was far from the only one. It was just that in my case, for a while I really thought it might last a little longer. But I soon knew he had other fish to fry – opera singers with an eye for youth, like Fiona, who could help his career on; principals' wives... I never told him I was pregnant. And I'm certain nobody had any idea who the father was. I wouldn't tell any of my tutors or the Principal."

"Why not?" said Katie.

"Things were different in those days," said Ginny. "I had the idea that I shouldn't do anything to wreck his career. He was the great violinist who could go to the very top, while I was the competent, uninspired pianist who could scratch a few pounds teaching pupils. But I've had secret thoughts for years that if I'd told the truth then and risked his anger, Julian might still be alive now."

Katie thought: the inner circle again. Above the law because they had so much more talent than the rest and that gave them the right. Ginny saw the look in Katie's eyes and seemed to know what she was thinking.

"Yes," she said. "I really thought that those who were truly brilliant at their music – especially if they were male – should get away with... I nearly said murder there. I don't believe it now. But that doesn't mean I wanted any revenge. I've been so happy all these years."

Sam looked at her mother without saying a word.

"Oh, yes," said Ginny. "I'm not just saying this because you're here or there's anything to hide or be ashamed of. The man I married was a lot older than me. He'd loved me for a long time before I went to the Conservatoire, but I'd ignored him. Now he was there again and he accepted what I'd done and stood by me. He offered me marriage, a home and a name for the baby and complete security. I accepted out of gratitude, but don't worry: I grew to love him. He was a wonderful husband and a wonderful father and now he's dead. He *never* referred to this and in time I almost forgot it. All these people were phantoms from a buried past, until this week when they became real again."

She looked Katie full in the face.

"So you see," she said, "it had nothing to do with me."

Katie didn't answer. She was too ashamed.

"Sam, come here," said Ginny.

Sam stood by her.

"I want you to make things up with Katie and Dave," Ginny said. "I know why Katie thought what she did and why they both came here. They've been through quite a lot as well. Now, forget it. There's no need for you to be angry. I'm not."

Sam's anger had died. She held out her hand to Katie, who took it. Then she kissed her on the cheek.

"Sorry," she said.

"So am I," said Katie.

"And that goes for Roger too," said Ginny. "He's a good lad. You could do a lot worse."

Sam smiled. "I know," she said. "I'll see you tomorrow."

"Aren't you going off with them now?" said Ginny.

"No, Mum," said Sam. Her voice was full with happiness. "I want to stay here and talk to you."

The door was softly closed. The three were left in the corridor.

"Is Sam's mum telling the truth?" said Dave.

"Of course she is," Katie answered. "It *shines* out."

"Let's go back to my kitchen," said Roger. "I'll boil the kettle again."

Once there, Roger made mugs of coffee for him and Dave and hot chocolate for Katie.

"So where are we now?" said Dave. "Either the police are right and they've got the murderer or there's still someone else."

"Everybody says the inner circle thought they were above the law because they were better than anybody else," said Katie.

"We know that," said Roger.

"Yes, but let me think. We know Sam's mum had nothing to do with it, but if she had there could be two motives. One: revenge for Julian's death; two: jealousy because they all got to the top while she was kicked out."

"Yes, but she didn't," said Roger. "She said she didn't worry about her own career."

"But Sam's mum's an ordinary person. We're dealing with a nutter here. What about someone who wanted to be in the inner circle but who never got there – or someone who *was* in it but never made it afterwards and got so upset about seeing all the others have huge success? That person could get really resentful and jealous – enough, from what we know of this lot, to murder."

"Frank didn't," said Roger.

"I know, but Frank's a normal human being as well," said Katie. "Like I said, we're dealing with a nutter."

Katie was quiet again. She felt suddenly breathless. She knew she was on the verge of something big.

"Who didn't get a variation dedicated to him because Hugo never rated him?" she said. "Who was it who

206

Ginny said never made it? Who was in the inner circle and was there the night of the pact? Who's never been heard of since until this week? Bill Weston. He could have done the lot."

"If he's mad enough," said Roger.

"Really paranoid," said Dave.

"He's always *there*," said Roger. "Turned up at Gerry's one night, called in on Hugo the next three hundred miles away."

"He's tall enough to be the Bimmerman who ran away," said Dave. "Though I can't say I recognized him."

"Neither did I," said Roger. "But if you put it like that…"

"…it's obvious," said Dave.

"But is it?" Katie replied.

Suddenly, Gwen poked her head round the door of the kitchen.

"Hullo, you lot," she said. "Any left for me?"

"Is Hugo with you?" asked Katie.

"Oh, no. Gone off with Gerry and Bill, his long-lost friends, hasn't he? No doubt to share the contents of the well-stocked drinks cabinet in Gerry's flat."

Suddenly, Katie felt her stomach turn over.

"Gwen," she said. "Hugo's put himself in danger."

Quickly they told her of their views on Bill. Gwen listened without interrupting. Then she said, "We must go to Gerry's flat and see for ourselves."

Katie put her mug of chocolate down.

"Can we get in?" she said.

"*I* can," said Gwen. "And I'll vouch for you if anyone asks."

There was a new chill in the air outside. The skies had clouded over. Rain was close: the week's fine weather was ending. The walk from the Hall of Residence to the Conservatoire took ten minutes. The night porter in the lodge recognized Gwen and nodded when she said they were bound for the Principal's flat.

"You'll be joining Sir Gerald's party then, Miss Fenton," he said. "Sir Gerald has brought his other guests in already."

"Come on!" Gwen cried urgently and set off at a run across the Victorian courtyard full of doorways and three storeys of windows, most dark though a few were softly lit. Katie had a sudden strong feeling of being watched. Someone was skulking in the shadows of the doorways, surveying their headlong run. And more than just being watched. She felt, like a blast of hot air on her neck, waves of malevolent hatred directed straight at her. She shivered – then looked as best she could from side to side but saw nothing.

They ran through an archway to a modern block. Gwen rushed through the double doors and pressed the button for the lift. It whisked them to the top floor where they found themselves in a carpeted hallway.

"That's Gerry's door," said Gwen.

There was no noise from inside. The door was closed. Gwen rang the bell. No answer.

Katie had a sinking feeling of foreboding.

Gwen knocked on the door, then looked through the letterbox.

"The lights are on," she said. "But it's all quiet."

She gave the door a push. To their surprise it opened;

it had been left on the latch.

They all went inside.

Still no sound, though the hallway was lit and the sitting room door was ajar, showing lights beyond it.

They entered the sitting room.

Gwen put her hand to her mouth to prevent the scream which rose to her lips. Dave and Roger both turned pale but said nothing. Katie knew her feeling of foreboding was correct.

Hugo stood in the middle of the room. He was in a state of deep shock. His eyes did not seem to have registered the new arrivals. In his right hand he held a small revolver.

Beside the leather sofa was a small metal waste-bin. In it were ashes and scraps of burnt paper. Smoke curled upwards from it.

On the rug spread over the polished hardwood floor was the body of Sir Gerald Swordblade. He had been shot through the head.

Hugo spoke. His voice sounded slurred. He seemed more concerned with the waste bin than Gerry's body.

"He burnt my music. Before my eyes he burnt my music."

"But who killed Gerry?" cried Katie.

Hugo looked down, as if seeing the body for the first time.

"I did, of course," he said. "I'm the guilty one."

19

For a full minute, the silence was absolute.
Then Gwen dropped her hand from her mouth and her scream filled the room. She ran to Hugo and put her arms round him as if trying to warm him back into some sort of awareness.

"Now we've *got* to get the police," said Dave. He found a phone, dialled 999 and spoke shortly into it: "Principal's flat. Royal Conservatoire. Murder."

He put the phone down.

"Now what?" he said.

Shuddering, Kate made herself look at Gerry. Then she turned to Hugo.

"Hugo!" she shouted. "You've got to tell us what happened."

Hugo slowly moved his head to look at her. His eyes were dull. He swayed from side to side, hardly able to stand, but he kept tight hold of the gun.

"He burnt my music," he said. His voice was slow and flat. "He'd got the manuscript of the variations that were in my study. He put them in the bin and set light to them. He laughed. He said that's the way all my music would go. What did he mean?"

"Hugo, *who*?" Katie yelled.

"Who?" Hugo repeated, like a ventriloquist's dummy.

"This is no good," cried Roger. "He's drunk. He's nearly paralytic. He hasn't got a clue what's going on."

"I shot Gerry," said Hugo. "With this gun. I must have."

"Where did you get it?" said Katie.

"I killed Gerry with it. Bill said so."

"Give it to me," said Roger.

"Keep away!" shrieked Gwen, her arms still tight round him. "Can't you see the terrible state he's in?"

"Gwen," said Dave, "if he won't talk sense, the police will come here and arrest him for murder."

"Yes," said Hugo in the same slurred voice. "For murdering Gerry. They'll come for me. I'll deserve it."

Gwen was silent, as if considering Dave's remark. Then she took her arms away from Hugo, stepped back and slapped him hard twice round the face. Hugo blinked, put his hands to where red now suffused his dead pale cheeks, then seemed to notice everyone for the first time. He looked down at Gerry.

"Gerry's dead," he said. "Oh, God!"

"Did you do this?" said Gwen.

"I don't know – I can't think. I wouldn't. I couldn't. But why do I think I did?"

"You said Bill told you." Katie did not feel she was

answering Hugo's question.

"Oh, God, it's true!" he said. "I tried to think it hadn't happened. But I am guilty, aren't I? I brought everybody to where they are now, didn't I? It's all my fault for writing the variations, isn't it?"

"Did you shoot Gerry?" asked Katie gently.

"I don't know. I must think. But not here – not over my friend's body."

Gwen led them into the dining room. They pushed chairs back from the table and sat watching Hugo. He placed his head in his hands and was silent for some minutes. Gwen disappeared into the kitchen. Very soon she returned with a mug of steaming black coffee. Hugo sipped it and visibly sobered up.

At last he spoke.

"It's all such a blur," he said. "Bill came back with us. We were all friends together. We drank Gerry's whisky. Gerry and I were swigging it down – out of relief at everything seeming to be over, I suppose." Katie noticed three glasses, one empty whisky bottle and another half full on the table. "I should have noticed that Bill was hardly sipping at his. I suddenly realized I'd had far too much: I'm not a heavy drinker as a rule. And everything was going woozy. I couldn't see properly, I couldn't think straight. But I could see that Bill had changed."

"Could he have slipped something in your glass?" said Roger.

"Maybe. But Bill was starting this tirade against us. I may have been half seas over, but I can remember this. Such bile, such anger, such grudges laid up and nursed over the years! We'd got where we were on his shoulders, he told us. We hadn't deserved success because we were no better than he was and he knew full well we'd conspired to do him down. He said what proved it was that he didn't have a variation dedicated to him in the Little Musgrave piece. That showed what I thought of him. He'd been the victim of the inner circle just as much as Julian was. But during last week all the rest had paid the price and now it was our turn. We couldn't believe this. Gerry told him to be sensible and sit down and Bill said, 'There you go again, Gerry, patronizing as ever,' and then he turned to me. *I* was the really guilty one in all this. *I* was responsible for the deaths of Laura and Alicia – yes, and Ronnie Stubbs too – and I was going to be guilty of the death of Gerry as well, all because I wrote those variations and woke up all the sleeping ghosts. And then he took cotton gloves out of his pocket and put them on. Then he pulled out a gun. And after that it all goes foggy. Gerry just stared at him, not saying a word, as if he was in deep shock. But I did hear Bill's voice saying something like, 'This is the final reckoning, Hugo. This is the peak of your guilt.' I managed to answer him. 'Bill,' I said, 'I know there's a bullet in there for me. And I know it must have been you who knocked me out on Thursday. Why didn't you finish me off then instead of just tapping me on the head and leaving me in the woods?' 'Who says I want to kill you?' he answered. 'There are plenty of other ways to destroy you.' Then he took a sheaf of papers from an inside pocket of his topcoat. I could see it was the first MS of the variations – the ones that were stolen. He dropped them in the waste bin and set light to them. He watched them burn and said, 'This gives me the purest pleasure of my life so far. All your music will go the same way now. After tonight you'll be discredited and soon you'll be forgotten. Except for this one thing: Hugo Malvern, the man who killed his friend.' And then it does all go into a complete blur. There was this loud crack in my ears and a sudden flash and a bitter smell like burning and Gerry was on the ground in front of me and Bill was gone and the gun was in my hand and it seemed stuck like glue so I couldn't get rid of it."

He had finished. Gwen's coffee had taken effect: Hugo looked clear-eyed and more composed. The others looked at each other, once again too shocked to speak.

"So Bill's plan must have been to ring the police, get them here and listen to you saying all that," said Roger.

"You'd have said, 'I'm guilty: I did it' when they arrrived, wouldn't you?" said Gwen.

"So they'd charge you straight away," said Dave. "Guilty on your own admission."

"That was an evil, daring plan," said Katie. "And it nearly worked."

At last Hugo put the gun down.

"They'd have found this still in my hand," he said.

"Bill put it there after he shot Gerry," said Gwen.

"I see that," said Roger. "And you see that. But will the police? What do they know about Bill Weston?"

"He was the intruder in your house, Hugo," said Katie.

"And the Bimmerman," said Roger.

"How long ago did all this happen?" asked Gwen.

"No idea," said Hugo.

"Not long," said Dave. "The paper in the bin's still smouldering."

And Katie *knew* it wasn't long. The unseen presence she felt watching them cross the courtyard was Bill Weston. He would realize that Gerry's murder would be discovered long before he intended, by people who would work out what had happened. So what would he do now a very clever plan had been foiled?

"Bill can't call the police now. He'll have to make a run for it," she said.

"In the Bimmer," said Roger. "But where will he go?"

"We'll clean Hugo's fingerprints off the gun," said Gwen.

"No, we won't," said Dave. "We touch nothing till the police come."

"So Bill killed all these people out of paranoid jealousy," said Gwen. "Murdered Laura, Alicia and Gerry and twisted things so Fiona and Hugo would be accused of their murders – all because they did better than him."

"It's a competitive world," murmured Katie.

"*And* found an accomplice and engineered his death as well. Don't forget Ronald Stubbs," said Dave.

Katie thought of something.

"The police will be here in a minute," she said. "Shouldn't Frank be told what happened?"

"Get him on the phone," said Dave.

"That's no good," said Katie. "He ought to be here in person. Someone will have to go and get him."

"We can't leave here," said Dave.

Katie made her mind up with that same impulsiveness which had taken her to Sussex the night before. "I'll go," she said. "One of us more or less won't matter. And I need some fresh air."

She also needed peace and quiet to think. All the questions were not answered yet. Before anyone could say "Not on your own," she was out of the door and in the lift.

Outside, she ran across the courtyard. As she passed the porter's lodge she looked through the door and shouted, "There's been some bother in the Principal's flat. The police are coming."

Before the porter could rise from his chair and stop her she was away, running down the empty street past the Citadel Centre and into the Hall of Residence.

The whole building was silent. Frank, like everyone else with any sense, would be on his own. Which room was it? Yes, she knew – the Warden's flat on the ground floor.

She hammered on the door.

"Oh, not again!" came a bleary voice. "Wait a minute."

The door opened. Frank stood there in dressing gown and pyjamas, looking angry.

"Can't I get a minute's rest?" he said. "No sooner has Liz woken me up saying some relative's dying and she's been called away urgently, than you of all people turn up. Well, what's the matter now?"

Katie poured out her story. The words tumbled over each other. Frank listened quiet and grim-faced throughout. When she finished, she half-expected him to say, "You've been trouble ever since we started this tour."

Instead he said, "Wait here. I'll get some clothes on and come back with you."

The door closed. Katie stood alone, thinking. She found herself wondering about one thing Frank had told her – that Liz had just been called away to a dying relative. Hard luck, Liz!

Then, suddenly and in the same curious way as before, came that odd vision of Christmas and the concert rehearsals last year. Why did it keep swimming unbidden into her mind? The picture was clear. A white car was parked some way off under a lamp. Liz came out of the Music Centre, saw Katie, said, "Good night. Well played," and walked towards it. Someone had got out, stepped round to the other side and was opening the passenger door for Liz. As they met, Katie was sure they kissed. Then the car started and drove off.

The someone in Liz's life. A tall male figure. *And Katie was certain who it was: Bill Weston.*

No, that was silly. A fleeting glimpse in the dark eight months ago, dimly recalled? She was putting him in her remembrance because he was so much on her mind.

No, she wasn't. *He was there*. She *had* seen Bill Weston before and it was with *Liz*.

But they didn't know each other. There had not been the slightest flicker of recognition between them on the roof garden.

Yet she had seen that not only did they know each other but also they were on close terms.

What did this mean?

They were concealing an established relationship. Why?

Katie could think of only one reason. But the idea was ridiculous.

Was *Liz* the dark figure at the centre of the web who set programmes of murder in motion and laughed as she did so? Was it *Liz* who told Bill Weston exactly when and where to go and what to do? Quiet, unassuming, highly competent *Liz*, the best musician of them all?

But it couldn't be. She had no reason, no connection with these matters.

All right, let's have a process of elimination. It can't be Frank; it's now clear that it can't be Sam's mum; it would never be one of the orchestra; to think it would be Anita Smith or poor old Arthur Armitage is ludicrous. So there's only Liz left.

But why? Why?

Frank's door opened. He stood there in thick green jersey and grey trousers and said, "Right. Let's go."

Katie had to run to keep up with him. Even so, she managed to gasp out her question.

"Frank, do Liz and Bill Weston know each other?"

"How should I know?" said Frank. "Impossible, I should think."

"Well, I think they do," said Katie. "I saw them together last Christmas."

"You must be mistaken," Frank grunted.

"But if I'm not and Liz has been keeping it quiet, then she's involved as well," Katie persisted.

"I don't believe it. I won't listen to you." Frank was angry.

They were approaching the Royal National Conservatoire. Police cars, their blue lights blinking, surrounded the entrance. A policeman stopped them as they approached.

"No one allowed past this point," he said.

"But we must," said Frank.

"I was one of those who called you," said Katie. "Sir Gerald Swordblade's been murdered."

The policeman looked keenly at her, then talked into his handset. A crackly answer came, then he talked again. When he had finished he spoke to Katie and Frank.

"Stay here. The inspector will want to talk to you both."

Then he turned away and seemed to forget them. Frank stood still, tapping his foot on the ground with irritation. Katie felt frustrated for a while, then began thinking once again about this new revelation.

Liz was the mastermind. But why? And where had she now gone? That story she told Frank was a lie. Liz had left in a hurry.

What made her go? Well, if Liz was at the centre she had to be able to communicate with Bill Weston at any time. Easy enough by mobile phone. Why shouldn't Liz have one? But the plan was obviously for Bill to disappear quietly after murdering Gerry, leaving Hugo in a state of shock with his fingerprints all over the murder weapon, and for Liz to sit tight. Perhaps months later everyone would hear how Liz and Bill became partners after a chance meeting where they recalled their brief but strange encounter on the tour. Out of misery comes happiness.

So why not wait?

Katie remembered again the feeling of being watched as they crossed the courtyard. Bill knew Gerry's murder would be discovered at once, that the essential time interval was gone and the circumstantial case against Hugo would disappear.

So he rang Liz and they decided – what?

Well, that was a theory and it could be right. How could she prove it? Because, despite the word of Gwen, Dave, Roger and herself, things could still be bad for Hugo. The police didn't have to believe them.

If only, thought Katie, *I could get into Liz's room. If she went in a hurry, incriminating things might be left.*

How could she? It would be locked. Well, the key should be with the porter. They'd all been told to give their keys back first thing tomorrow morning. If she slipped back now, she could tell the porter Liz had asked her to go into the room and pick up a few things she'd forgotten.

It was worth trying. And after all, as far as individual excursions were concerned, for all this week she'd been on a roll. She made her mind up. *She would cut back to the Hall of Residence and search Liz's vacated room.*

The policeman wasn't looking. Frank was miles away and never noticed her. Now was the time.

She slipped away unnoticed, round a corner into a narrow street which doubled back into the main street about fifty metres further on. Then she walked quickly towards the Hall of Residence and past the Citadel Centre.

Her thoughts were busy again.

What could Liz's connection be with the murders, with the inner circle, Laura, Alicia, Gerry, Hugo? Liz never went to the Conservatoire.

So she couldn't have been one of Julian's many conquests. She showed no recognition of either Hugo or Gerry, or they of her. She remained the great outsider. But there must be a connection. It couldn't be that she was just infected by Bill's insane jealousy.

No, there must be something else – something which happened years ago, before all this started.

She cudgelled her brains.

What could it be?

Something so *simple*…

She let her mind go blank as her footsteps echoed in the deserted street. Odd scenes from the past week dropped idly into her mind: yesterday's chase across London, seeing Gerry for the first time in the close at Wardminster, talking with Gwen under the tree in the small hours of Monday morning, listening to her brother Ricky excitedly telling her over the phone of Laura's murder…

Of course! Got it! So perfectly *right* that it must be true.

Julian Stubbs was Liz's brother!

It had to be. Would that be enough to start such a campaign of revenge?

It could, if Liz was sure a murder had been done and no one was called to account for it.

She had turned left down another street by now and was passing the entrance to the main car parks of the Citadel Centre. A car was just coming through the automatic barrier and she walked past without looking.

But if Liz was Julian's sister, that meant something very odd indeed.

The car drove slowly along behind her, then stopped. A door opened and quietly closed again.

Katie's sudden thought was so amazing as to be almost funny. She found herself saying it aloud.

"If Julian Stubbs was Liz's brother, that means Liz is Sam's auntie!"

A hand closed with a grip of steel over her arm. A voice in her ear hissed, "Well done, Katie! Got it in one."

The voice was that of Liz herself. Before Katie could cry out, another hand was clamped over her mouth and she was roughly turned round. By the kerb in front of her stood a white BMW and at the wheel was Bill Weston. He leant over and opened the rear door.

The faces of neither were welcoming. Katie knew, as Liz shoved her into the back and sat beside her, still clasping her arm, that she had walked into a sudden and complete trap and she was alone with two paranoid murderers.

20

The inspector – the same man who had arrested Fiona on the roof garden – had already commandeered a large practice studio as his incident room. Gwen, Dave, Roger and now Frank sat outside it while Hugo was inside being questioned.

"Where's Katie?" demanded Dave.

Frank looked guilty.

"I've no idea," he replied. "One minute we were waiting together; the next she had just disappeared."

"I don't like it," Dave muttered. "We'd better tell someone."

A sergeant opened the door.

"All in here, please," he said. "The inspector wants to speak to you."

They filed in. The inspector – large, florid with crinkly hair, wearing a dark suit – spoke in a level, equable voice.

"I have to say," he said, "that I find it strange you were so soon on hand after this murder was committed. However, we'll discuss that later. After this evening's events on the roof garden and from enquiries made by other police forces, I know this murder is not a one-off. And while I don't necessarily accept it, I am sufficiently impressed by Mr Malvern's version of what happened to want to speak to Mr Weston at once. Now, where is he likely to be?"

They all looked at each other helplessly. Then Roger spoke.

"In his white BMW," he said.

"Roger, you can't be sure it's his," said Gwen.

"Don't be daft! Of course it is," Roger answered.

"Registration number?" asked the Inspector.

Dave and Roger looked at each other.

"It's personalized," said Dave.

"And it nearly makes a word something to do with music," said Roger.

"Thanks," said the inspector. His voice was so even they couldn't tell if he was being sarcastic. "It's a start. Get on to it," he continued to a WPC who left the room at once.

Frank now cleared his throat and spoke.

"Inspector, there's something I have to tell you, though it hurts me and makes me feel disloyal."

The rest stared at him.

"Before Katie Summers – not for the first time – went off on her own just now, she told me something I refused to believe. She said Bill Weston knew my assistant, Mrs Woolley, at least eight months ago and they didn't seem casual acquaintances then."

The others stared at each other.

"Nobody had any idea of this, least of all me. But tonight, just at the time the murder was discovered, Mrs Woolley came to me saying she had been called away urgently. Someone in her family was dying. These two things coming together are so striking that I have to tell you."

"I'm sorry," said the inspector. "I don't want to appear dim, but what precisely are you telling me?"

"That Liz Woolley, my trusted assistant of several years, is in partnership with the man you're looking for."

"Partnership is rather jumping the gun, sir, if I may say so. We are on the point of charging one person already tonight with murder and we have a prime suspect for the latest."

Frank looked sick. The thought that if Liz were innocent, Fiona and Hugo would go down for murder was not to his liking.

"What's more to the point, sir, is if you could give us some idea of where our two runaways – *if* they are together in the BMW you mention – might be heading."

Dave felt a sinking of the heart. "They've got Katie," he said. "I *know* it!"

Katie was squashed up against the side of the car. Something was digging in her ribs, which felt suspiciously like the barrel of a gun. Liz's face was very close to hers.

"What a timely coincidence seeing you," she said. "An opportunity heaven-sent."

"For what?" Katie gulped.

"For the second reckoning of the evening," Liz replied. "It's only *you* who wrecked things for us. Only *you* crept nearer and nearer the truth, never letting go, always lurching on to the next stage, no matter what we did to stop you. Now, finally, you spoil our grand finale before we drift off into obscurity and happy domesticity."

Katie said nothing. A presentiment, heavy as lead, of what was coming shortly forced itself on her. But there was something else. Liz was angry. She shook with such rage as to make little eddies of disturbance in the air. Surely, having so coincidentally captured her greatest scourge, she should be triumphant.

"You see," said Liz, her voice shaking dangerously, "we shouldn't be making a midnight flit like this. Gerry should have been disposed of in *my* time –" why not *our* time? Katie wondered – "and Hugo with him. But no. I have a fool as a partner who thinks because he is so high on killing after his wonderful week that he can walk on water. He thinks he can act on his own without telling me. Look where it's landed us."

Katie realized the object of Liz's anger was not her at all, but Bill. Meanwhile, he had restarted the BMW and they were moving smoothly through unfamiliar streets.

"It never seemed to occur to him that Hugo might actually *remember* that he didn't kill Gerry and that it was my so-called lover who put the gun in his hand and *told* him he had."

Bill spoke. His voice was almost pleading.

"It *would* have worked," he said. "I left Hugo standing over Gerry with a still-smoking gun. When the police came he would have said straight away, 'I did it.' He would because I told him to and I *had* his mind then. I *did*. I was just going to call the police anonymously. They would have found him and he would have incriminated himself straight away. My love, don't you see? We would have got *three on the same night*!"

"But we didn't," said Liz grimly. "The meddling little crew got there first and they soon snapped our Hugo out of it, I'll be bound. *Didn't you?*" This last she hissed in Katie's ear.

Dumbly, Katie nodded.

"So we're on the run," said Liz. "Needlessly. But when this clown rings me I know I've got to go with him because I daren't let him be captured alone. We sink or swim together. Tough, isn't it? But why worry? We have a little friend we can sink with now, haven't we, Katie?"

Once again, Katie didn't answer. She knew exactly what Liz meant.

"Until the time comes when I have to silence you, you can be our passport to safety."

"A hostage?" Katie blurted out.

"If you like," said Liz. "Except that hostages sometimes end up free. You won't, I'm afraid. Sorry, but you know too much already."

Katie felt sick. Nausea spread through her. Liz meant it. So this was where the path had led to. *Why* had she meddled? There was no way out of this. Nobody knew where she was; the others didn't even know that now she was supposed to be begging the key off the porter to look through Liz's room. Instead she'd worked out nearly everything for herself and she'd been right. And how she wished she wasn't.

But there was so much she didn't know – not that she could really care less now. Though she had a shrewd idea that these two psychopaths were going to tell her. After all, Liz had nearly, in her own eyes, brought off a triumph. It was unlikely that she wouldn't want to share it with *somebody*, even if the likely life expectancy of that somebody was now pretty short.

And besides, there was a nugget of hope to cling on to. She was in a white BMW and Dave and Roger would tell the police about it. This was a little piece of pure gold she could keep to herself, take out, look at and polish whenever another wave of hopeless horror swept over her.

Meanwhile, she *must* know the rest – for her own satisfaction.

"Why all this, Liz?" she said. "Why? Julian died a long time ago."

She still half-expected a hiss of, "Shut up!" But no. Liz started speaking. *I was right about her*, Katie thought.

"What's that got to do with it? You know *nothing*. There were three of us – kids in Birmingham. Our father had run off and our mother was on social security. God knows why she so wanted us all to do music! Julian had a broken child's violin begged off a junk shop and before he was six everybody knew he was a prodigy. Our mum did everything she could to get us where she thought we ought to be: when Julian got into the Conservatoire at eighteen she really thought she could die happy. And she did, not long after. But I knew she wanted me to follow Julian. And I was going to. I was determined on that. Poor Ronnie, though! The encouragement had gone by the time he was old enough to think about it. No good to

228

anyone was Ronnie. But well able to grieve for his brother when the time came."

Liz paused. *Don't stop!* Katie was willing her on.

"By the time he got there, Julian was a sublime violinist. He'd have got to the top all right." Her voice had shaken with affection; now it hardened into malevolence. "And they killed him because he was too good for them, because they feared him for his strength that they didn't have, because they resented that someone from a class they despised had struggled for what they got so easily. And they all came to his funeral, those *cheats*, those *hypocrites*, those *murderers* – Fiona Tankerton, Laura Merchant, Alicia Vernon, Gerry Swordblade, Hugo Malvern, Ken Vanstone – with their sad, hangdog, guilty faces."

"But Fiona said his death was accidental," said Katie.

"I *don't care* what Fiona said!" screamed Liz. "She may be right. It doesn't matter. What matters is, *that's what they wanted*, all of them."

"All?" said Katie, looking at the back of Bill's head as he drove without attempting to join in.

"I'm beginning to wonder whether I have to add him to the list after all," said Liz. "I could see their collective guilt but I watched unobserved and I saw one face that was different. Critical, sardonic – even then, I liked it. Bill's. I was drawn to that face. He wouldn't know, though, for years yet."

Katie risked a glance out of the window. They were in an indistinguishable part of London. A large green road sign flashed by – A12 *Colchester*. Bill Weston drove steadily. For a murderer attempting escape and facing the unpredictable ire of his accomplice he seemed remarkably composed.

Liz continued.

"It was then I knew I had to avenge Julian's needless death. I saw something different in another face that day. There was fear in the eyes of the snivelling Ken Vanstone. A weak link, I thought. I wrote asking him to meet me in London. He came, shifty and scared as always. I'd slipped a knife in my bag in case he turned out tougher than I thought. I needn't have worried. I wormed half the stuff out of him with no trouble. He was there the night of the fire, with Fiona, but he wouldn't admit to murder. He made me so angry, that little turn-coat! Not fit to live, I thought. Then I realized that perhaps after all I hadn't brought the knife to defend myself with. There was another use for it. We were crossing Regent's Park. It was dark. I had to catch my train home from Euston. He was getting on my nerves. So I slipped the knife between his ribs so easily: he dropped at once without a sound. I took his wallet and burned it as soon as I got home. And I found out how easy it was for people like us to kill. I kept that thought in my mind for many years to come."

Katie couldn't believe this.

"*You* killed him?" she gasped. "Frank's worked all these years with the murderer of his best friend?"

Liz laughed.

"Nice, isn't it?" she said. "Wouldn't he be surprised?"

The sickness in Katie's heart hurt even more.

"I never went to the Conservatoire," said Liz. "I wouldn't. I got a place at university instead, where I could work without distraction and watch from afar. I'd started my revenge, but it wasn't time yet to complete it. After all, as much pleasure comes in the contemplation of a deed as in the doing of it. My time would come: I knew that. Watch and wait – while I trained, I taught, I married and divorced. When I came to work with Frank – what a heaven-sent opportunity – I knew the time was close."

"But didn't Frank know who you were?"

"Why should he? Hedfordshire's an Equal Opportunities employer. There's not even space on the application form for a maiden name. But I had no grudge against Frank. I knew he wasn't involved, though I also knew that sooner or later he would lead me to my quarries. Then one day, on a course I attended, I saw a face I knew – sharp, quizzical, ruthless, embittered, like mine. Of course! Bill Weston, lame duck of the inner circle."

Bill spoke as he drove.

"Less of the lame duck, my darling."

"Only joking, sweetheart," Liz replied. "Bill and I got talking. Didn't we, my love?" That question was uttered very loud and clear, as if expecting an answer. Bill nodded and murmured, "As you say," and Liz continued. "And we soon found out how much we had in common. Hatred of the inner circle united us. Oh, how that brought us together! Soon, we knew we'd do *anything* for each other. Wouldn't we, my love?" Another nod and "As you say." "So, bound together secretly – for no one, least of all Frank, must know of our union – we waited."

"But I saw you at Christmas, after the rehearsal," said Katie.

Well, why shouldn't Liz know they had let their guard slip just once – but fatally?

"You see?" said Liz. "I told you to stay in the car."

"Silly me!" said Bill. His right hand stayed on the steering wheel as he slapped it playfully with his left.

"I knew the sign to start our revenge would be unmistakable," said Liz. "And, sure enough, it came."

"How should I know where they'll go?" said Frank.

"Where does Mrs Woolley live?" said the inspector.

"She'd hardly go there," said Frank.

"We must check," said the inspector.

Frank gave a Hedford address.

"I can't help with Weston," said Hugo. "I haven't a clue where he lives now."

"There must be a place they'd go to," said the inspector to Frank. "*Think*, sir. *Think!*"

Liz continued.

"I'll never forget the day Frank said he would commission Hugo to write for the orchestra. I hope I hid my delight with suitable awe. Then Hugo told us what he was writing. Had I sent someone to tell him, like the mysterious stranger who ordered a requiem from Mozart, he could not have provided anything better. I knew then that fate was on my side. And I also realized that we weren't the only ones who remembered these events. Guilt runs deep."

"Only for some, my love," said Bill. "Only for some."

"So we planned the shape of our revenge. Me to control from the centre; Bill to act – to kill, to set one against the other, to kill again. Then came a complication. Ronnie came out of prison, as welcome as smallpox. He saw we were on to something. He was an embarrassment. But we didn't dare rebuff him: he could make trouble for us. Besides, he was once as grief-stricken over his brother's death as I was. So we used him. I found him a task. I had followed Hugo's career closely and I knew all about Gwen Fenton. I saw that she was in Leeds so I sent Ronnie there with a riddling message for Hugo guaranteed to scare him stiff. And then Ronnie was to stay out of the way for a while until I needed him again."

Katie remembered the sprawling, broken body. Needed him for what?

"And then, while Hugo and Gerry satisfyingly blamed each other, we started on our campaign. We could keep in touch, Bill and I. We had mobile phones. We could talk direct – or, when that was too dangerous, I could ring my own home and leave a message on the answering machine for Bill to call up and hear at any time. Our communication never failed. So to the first, easy murder: Laura. We knew where she was and, to the minute, when her variation was played. Perfect timing, for maximum effect."

Katie couldn't help bursting out.

"But Laura had done *nothing*!"

"She was one of them. She had put her hand to a bond. She closed ranks with the others. That was enough."

"So why not kill Gerry in Yorkshire on Tuesday? That's what we thought had happened. Why wait till tonight?"

Even as she spoke, the full horror of what she had so recently seen in the Principal's flat was beginning to sink in.

"Because his time had not yet come. He had to be used first. Our plan was more subtle than mere butchery. These people vowed unity once and we had to set one against the other. We prepared poison for Bill to pour in Gerry's ear. Besides, it was little more than the actual truth. Fiona was at the fire that night and we could incriminate her in Laura's murder. But Gerry turned up unexpectedly at Wardminster on Monday. We nearly panicked. Had he changed his plans? No, I overheard him and could tell Bill where he would be – to the minute."

"So Gerry was convinced Fiona was a murderer," said Katie. "But what if everybody knew where she was on Monday night?"

"You forget," said Liz. "There's another figure in this equation: Ronnie. More about him later."

"There must be lots more figures in it," said Katie. "Who went to Amsterdam?"

"That was so easy. Bill drove Gerry south through the night. He dropped him in London, went to the City Airport and walked straight on a plane for Amsterdam – no long drawn-out formalities there. Unlike Hugo, we knew Alicia was touring with the PPO. Bill rang Alicia before he left London. By the time he landed at Schiphol Airport she was there to meet him. He'd hired a car in advance. He only needed three hours in Amsterdam to finish the job. Alicia's at the bottom of a canal and Bill was back in London ringing to see what message was left for him on the machine. Amazing news. Hugo had gone to Alicia's rescue like some shining knight. Well, that was Bill's destination solved. Find Hugo, follow him, meet him and set him up with the same poison about Fiona."

"None of which is true," said Katie.

"It is. She killed Julian. From that, all else springs."

"She says she didn't."

"I say she did."

"But nobody could ever prove it. She'll go on trial and be let off. That's no revenge."

"Oh, no," said Liz. "She'll be tried for murder. And found guilty, I promise you."

"Whose murder?"

"Ronnie's."

"Did she?"

"I said Ronnie was as welcome as smallpox. He had no idea Bill had left scraps of evidence at Laura's house to suggest he'd been there. The police will soon be sorting out what they are. Ronnie turned up again on Wednesday night, anxious to be of service to big sister. Well, I had a use for him. I told him to meet me next day in London: not at the Citadel Centre..."

"Of course!" Katie gasped. "The Science Musuem."

She remembered the tantalizing flash of light blue. And what had Liz worn that day, starting with the uncomfortable interview in the morning? Faded, washed-out blue jeans.

"Correct," said Liz. "Ronnie arrived, certain he was followed. I knew at once who by. So his first job was to be sure you would never follow anyone again. He failed, as you know. But his main job was to break into Fiona's flat

– burglary was his real talent. Bill would meet him outside and together, Ronnie thought, they would plant evidence against her. So Ronnie got them in, then Bill did the business Ronnie didn't bargain for. He heaved him over the balcony, then came outside and watched Fiona return with no idea she'd been burgled or what lay on the pavement below. By now, the police will have found everything they need to accuse her of Ronnie's murder. No one will doubt that the hefty Fiona could make short work of an undersized runt like my younger brother. And there'll be more in the flat to connect Ronnie with Laura. So they'll say Fiona used him to kill for her and that, in the end, thieves fall out."

Katie couldn't speak. There was no escape, no hope. She was alone with monsters.

"Did Mrs Woolley have nothing in her life besides her job?" the inspector persisted.

Frank was thinking hard. Something dawned.

"There's one possibility," he said.

Bill had steered the BMW away from the main road. Outside was dark, empty countryside. Katie shivered. She was lost. The end was near.

Bill was speaking now. He had turned to look at Liz.

"You must let me tell her my part of the scheme," he said.

"Watch the road!" snapped Liz.

Katie remembered Roger's account of being cut up by the BMW near Hugo's. Perhaps, however impressive his car, Bill wasn't that good a driver. The road was narrow.

The BMW lurched at corners where they were taken too fast.

"You can tell when I've finished," Liz went on. "Yours is nothing to brag about." Yes, Liz was the stronger by far.

Katie still had the power of thought despite her despair. She knew it was all that could save her.

"How could Bill be everywhere at once? He was at Hugo's in the morning, Fiona's in the afternoon and back at Hugo's in the evening," she said.

"Thursday was not my darling's finest hour, was it?" There was a dangerous edge to Liz's voice. "I didn't ask him to rifle Hugo's study for the Musgrave manuscript. That was his idea only. And when I realized our tiresome detective was on the move again – listening to your friends finding out Hugo's address in the theatre showed me where you and Gwen had gone – I sent him back to Sussex to try a second attempt to silence you." She spoke to Bill again. "That was a disaster, wasn't it?"

Bill said nothing. His fingers showed white as he gripped the steering wheel too hard.

"I know pyromania is the least of your vices," Liz said to him. "And I know that for this affair to begin and end with blazing houses and trapped victims would have a certain symmetry. But I'm so *glad* you were seen and had to run for it. Getting away unrecognized meant you could delay our real disaster a full twenty-four hours." By now, the sarcasm in her voice felt like razor blades even to Katie. How must Bill be taking it?

Bill did not answer. He stepped harder on the accelerator and braked violently at a bend.

A slight salt smell drifted into the car. Katie knew they were near the sea.

"The Blackwater!" Frank cried. "Of course. She has a motor-cruiser moored there. On the Crouch estuary near Burnham. Besides music, it's her great love."

The inspector turned to the sergeant.

"Get on to the Essex police," he said. "Full description of car; two, perhaps three, occupants. Tell them we may have a hostage situation. By now they could be between Chelmsford and Burnham. I want them caught."

"But then, Bill," said Liz. "You have a strange scale of priorities. I suppose burning a few scraps of paper in front of Hugo meant more to you than anything else."

"And why not?" said Bill defiantly. "Destroying things of the mind is far worse than destroying the body.

"Ah!" replied Liz. "But while my hatred ennobles me, your jealousy corrodes you. So you overreached yourself and you've nearly done for us both."

Oh, they're never going to have an abstract discussion about purity of motive at this stage of the game? Obscurely, the thought gave Katie hope.

Bill's voice rose.

"I've *killed* for you this week! I won't have you mock my own triumph."

"Sometimes you're like a child," Liz retorted.

The road was rougher now and Katie could tell that a wide expanse of water was very close. Bill was driving even faster; he was angry.

"We're hooked to each other now, like it or not," he shouted.

Whatever they did to make it seem as though Fiona and Ronnie fell out was happening now for real, thought Katie. Her glimmer of hope strengthened slightly.

"I gave you no leave to kill Gerry!" Liz shrieked. "He should have been left to me in my own time."

Katie felt the car jerk violently as Bill braked too hard into a bend.

"You don't understand!" he shouted.

"Oh, yes, I do." Liz's voice was quieter. "I should never have depended on you. Your judgement failed us both."

Bill didn't answer. Katie could see he was no longer leaning back in his seat, steering straight-armed like a confident rally driver. He was hunched forward, straining at the wheel, movements jerky. She knew he was going too fast for the next bend. She waited for what had to happen. There was a violent squeal of brakes – too late. The stomach-wrenching deceleration hurled Katie forward, and only the seat-belt kept her from crashing into the headrest of the front seat. The BMW skidded, plunged into the grass verge, seemed to lift into the air, then headed downwards in a split-second dive which seemed to Katie to last an eternity. She tried to brace herself for a final neck-breaking collision with the ground.

But instead the car hit the side of the drainage ditch it had landed in, careered wildly from side to side with the windows suddenly opaque with spray, then came to rest in flowing water.

239

The silence was overpowering. For a moment, Katie didn't dare try to move. Then, gently, she flexed all her limbs and muscles. Amazingly, she seemed all right. She undid her safety-belt and sat up.

Liz was slumped beside her, not moving. What should she do? Try to run for it? The door on her side had burst open. Cautiously, she started to creep through it.

The same vice-like grip as before closed over her arm.

"Oh, no, you don't!" Liz's voice. "We're not done yet."

With her other hand, Liz reached forward and touched Bill Weston on the shoulder. He was sprawling forwards, his head on the steering wheel. For a moment, Katie thought he was dead.

"I've a good mind to end him here," said Liz. "Put him out of his misery."

Bill groaned, lifted his head, straightened up. There was a livid bruise and blood on his forehead.

"Satisfied?" said Liz. "So much for your lovely BMW."

"Now what?" said Bill. He seemed beaten, completely dominated by Liz.

"Torch the car," Liz replied. "You'll not need it again. Anyone who sees the flames will think it's joyriders."

Bill struggled out of his seat and stepped knee-deep into cold water. He swayed once or twice, then seemed to pull himself together, as if the shock of cold water had brought him round. Then he leant back into the car, felt in the glove compartment and brought out a large yellow cleaning cloth. "Get out and get ready to run," he said.

Liz scrambled out into the water, Katie followed and

Liz pushed her up the bank. Bill gripped Liz's hand while he steadied himself, legs wide, on the slope of the bank and took a cigarette lighter out of his pocket. Then, arms extended to full reach, he leaned out, undid the petrol-filler cap, stuffed the cloth in the vent, flicked the lighter on and applied it to the cloth. Liz pulled him up over the top and they all three staggered away down the road. The sudden "*crump!*", the yellow light and searing heat and the blast of the explosion followed them not half a second afterwards. By that time they were running, Liz still dragging Katie by the hand.

After a hundred metres they stopped, breathless. Katie looked back. An orange mass of flames still danced. She looked the other way. For the first time she could take stock of her surroundings.

They were standing on a rough road through grazing land covered by drainage ditches. Except for a few drops in the cold wind blowing from nearby water, the night was fine though dark with cloud. She smelt salt again and was aware of an empty vastness close by. They had reached the sea.

She looked the other way. All was dark and featureless. A few isolated lights far off showed where farmhouses were. There was no comforting glow from a town.

She was on her own. She was finished.

The four waiting for news from the inspector were disappointed.

Nothing. The search for Katie round the Conservatoire, back at the Hall of Residence and throughout the Citadel Centre and the surrounding streets had yielded nothing. And no white BMWs were reported heading east towards moored motor cruisers.

Anyway, why would they want to go for a sail at a time like this?

Liz dragged Katie along. Bill loped in front, showing no ill-effects from hitting his head on the steering wheel. Katie's eyes were now used to the dark. She saw they were away from grass, ditches and grazing cattle. The road was a mere track with salt marshes on either side. They were approaching a tidal creek.

Katie was past wondering why.

Now they were beside lapping water. A wooden jetty ran out and the tide was in. At the far end bobbed an old motor cruiser – hardly fit to anchor off Monte Carlo but stubby, stout and serviceable all the same.

They stopped. Katie looked at the boat.

"Last resort," said Liz.

She pushed Katie along the jetty. Katie resisted.

"I shouldn't if I were you," said Liz. "I can end it all here so easily."

Katie said nothing, but started to shuffle along the jetty. Close to the cruiser, Liz stopped and held her back.

"Take a good look from the outside," she said. "You've brought this on yourself. The boat has been ready here for months: false passports, new clothing, everything to change our identities and start a journey to miles away, beyond police, beyond extradition. And we never thought we'd have to use it. Until you came along and meddled and dear Bill here puts a foot wrong and makes it too risky for us to stay and tough it out. Well, Katie, this will be your last home."

Katie couldn't speak. She suddenly wanted to scream, but who would hear her? And besides, Liz still had the gun in her hand.

Liz continued.

"We'll slip across the North Sea. We'll be off the coast of Holland by morning. Into the dinghy we'll get, everything we need packed on it. We'll slip ashore unnoticed at some lonely spot, but the cruiser will be no more. We'll have scuttled it before we leave and it will never be found. And you'll go down with it, Katie, and they'll never find you either."

The last ray of hope was extinguished.

The inspector entered.

"They've got something!" he said. "Come on."

Bill clambered into the cruiser and went to the wheel. Liz pushed Katie after him and slipped the mooring ropes. The engine burst into burbling life. The gap between the boat and jetty widened.

Katie took a last hopeless look at the dark land she was leaving.

No, suddenly it was no longer dark. Cars were racing towards the jetty and fanning out so they were ranged along the side of the creek. There was a clatter in the air as a helicopter flew low over them.

Liz screamed. "How could they know?"

Bill turned from the wheel.

"Call *me* a fool?" he stormed. "I torched my beautiful car because you said so and look where it's got us!"

243

Katie watched, amazed and suddenly hopeful.

"Get back! Steer the boat!" Liz's voice was shrill, forced, unnatural. Katie saw an ugliness in her eyes more frightening than anything she had seen in her before.

Bill did no such thing.

"You can't blame me for this!" he yelled. "I blame you. I curse the day I met you."

Suddenly, all pretence at restraint between them was gone.

"Of course you do!" Liz shrieked. "I knew it. You may be twisted up with jealousy inside because you weren't as good as the others in the inner circle. But you're *still one of them*. I should never have forgotten that."

Katie looked back at the shore. Figures had emerged from the cars. Equipment was being pulled out of a Range Rover and suddenly a beam of light swept the creek. A voice crackled over the loudhailer.

"Make for the shore!"

Bill bellowed at Liz.

"It could never have worked."

"Steer the boat!" Liz screamed again.

But Bill continued to face her.

"We're finished because of you."

The loudhailer voice crackled again.

"Give yourselves up! Trained marksmen have you in their sights."

"Do they indeed!" said Liz. She seized Katie again. Despite Katie's struggles, Liz was too strong for her. She dragged Katie after her, up on to the cabin roof, in full sight of the police on the shore, then caught her in a choking grip round the neck, pushed her round so she became a shield and shouted at her pursuers.

"Now let's see how good your marksmen are!"

The loudhailer voice came again.

"Release the girl!"

"No chance!" Liz answered. "If I go down, we all go."

"Perhaps some of us don't want to go down," Bill's voice came from below.

Liz looked down on him.

"That's you all over, isn't it? That's how it's been all the time. At heart you were always one with those you killed. People like me and Julian and even poor Ronnie – you despise us, don't you?"

Bill, without a word, turned back to the wheel.

Liz spoke again. Not a shriek now, but a high, carrying voice which must have carried easily and thrillingly to the watchers on the shore. Pressed up so close as she was, Katie could feel the strength of a trained voice in Liz's opening and closing lungs. It was an awesome sensation.

"There's one verse of Little Musgrave that you've all forgotten, but it's what this is all about. I'm going to sing it to you."

And now, in this final nightmarish, almost unearthly encounter, Katie heard words she never expected to hear again, sung steadily, oddly beautifully, in a voice produced not six inches from her ear:

"'A grave, a grave,' Lord Barnard cried,
'To put these lovers in.
But lay my lady on the upper hand,
For she comes of the better kin.'"

* * *

Bill looked up at her. His eyes glinted fearlessly.

"Well, Liz, if that's how you see things, so be it. Laura, Alicia, Gerry – I've murdered them all for you. Yet they're all worth ten of you."

They continued to look at each other. Then there was a sharp crack, so close as to fill Katie's ears stingingly, and an acrid smell of cordite. Bill lay sprawled in the well of the boat, blood seeping from his chest.

There was another popping motor-boat noise. A police inflatable launch approached. The loudhailer voice was very clear.

"Give up now!"

"Not while I have Katie," Liz answered.

Katie could see the launch not fifty metres away, gaining fast. Suddenly, she wondered how the cruiser she was on could keep going forward now its helmsman was dead.

The answer came at once. The boat had sailed unsteered too long through a twisting channel marked by buoys. Without warning a jarring shock ran through it and it lurched on to its port side, aground. Suddenly, the grip round Katie's neck was loosened: she and Liz were falling. The guard rails round the cabin roof crashed bruisingly into her right thigh as she slithered helplessly into the cold, choking water. She never saw Liz lose her grip, stagger on the suddenly sloping roof, throw up her hands and, all balance lost, topple into the water with hardly a splash.

The police launch was here. Strong arms reached down and pulled Katie up and on board. Nearby, Liz was